For Want of a Father

Hazel Hart

Cover design by B.J. Myrick
Old Cowtown stagecoach cover photo taken by Hazel Hart
Permission to use the Old Cowtown stagecoach granted by
Old Cowtown Museum, Wichita, Kansas

ISBN: 1533521425
ISBN-13: 978-1533521422

DEDICATION

Carly

ACKNOWLEDGMENTS

Thank you to my critique partners, B.J. Myrick, Victoria Hermes-Bond, and Wes Brummer, who made many valuable suggestions during the writing of this book. Special thanks go to B.J. Myrick for designing the book cover and Victoria Hermes-Bond for her help with researching nineteenth-century fashions.

1) A LETTER FROM AMBROSE

Lucy

Westport, Missouri
May, 1859

I was expecting my weekly letter from Ambrose, so I hovered around the hotel check-in desk, whisking my feather duster over knickknacks and sneaking looks at my sister Cordelia while she sorted the mail. Slowly, methodically, she organized the letters in stacks—the regular boarders', Grandma's, Aunt Hannah's, and business mail addressed to the hotel—and slid them into the row of cubbyholes behind the desk. Cordelia was being her usual spiteful self, making me wait because our brother addressed his letters to me instead of her, the older sister.

She frowned and studied the address on a small, letter-sized package about an inch thick. "For you," she said.

I dropped the duster, grabbed the package from her hand, and glanced at the return address. "It's from Ambrose!"

My fingernails clawed at the sealed wrapping. When at last I worked through the outer layer, something thudded to the floor. I picked up the hard, flat object and unfolded the paper around it.

"A twenty dollar gold piece!" I scanned the letter. "Ambrose says Pa wants me home. I'm to go on the next stage. This money is for my fare and whatever else I need." My deepest wish had at last come true. "I'm going home!"

My little sisters, Jennie and Ella, rushed in, their braids bouncing, and looked up at me, their brown eyes shining with excitement.

"What about us?" Ella, the nine-year-old, asked. "Do we get to go home, too?"

"Not now, but Ambrose says if I do a good job and prove I can take care of the house and you, too, Pa will send for you."

Ella ducked her head and squeezed seven-year-old Jennie's hand. "We'll never get to go. Pa thinks we're too much trouble."

"That's not it. He just wants to make sure I can take proper care of the house and you girls." I smiled and patted Ella's shoulder. "It won't take long for me to show Pa how much I've learned in the past four years about doing woman's work." Unable to contain my excitement, I waved my hands, shooing my little sisters from the room. "You girls go find Aunt Hannah. I have to tell her I'm leaving and start packing."

"We'll get her," Jennie said.

The two girls whirled and ran from the room, shouting, "Aunt Hannah, Aunt Hannah, come hear the news."

Cordelia's mouth was a straight line of disapproval as she fiddled with the pen, ink bottle and ledger on the check-in desk. "No need to hurry with the packing. There's not a stage heading west for two days."

Irritated by the implied criticism, I snapped, "I'm not a last-minute person. I plan what I do."

Cordelia was impulsive, changing from one minute to the next, acting on whims without thinking of how she affected others. Running away and leaving me, only nine years old at the time, alone to care for our sick mother was one of those actions I could never forgive. Ma might have lived if Cordelia hadn't taken off when she did.

Aunt Hannah's voice mingled with my little sisters' as they emerged from the hallway. Stopping in front of me, she tilted her head and frowned, her eyes narrowing. "What's this about you going home?"

I held up the letter and gold coin. "Ambrose said to come on the next stage. Pa sent twenty dollars to pay my way." I cast Cordelia a sour look before continuing to speak to Aunt Hannah. "I know you don't like Pa. He doesn't like you, either. But he's my pa, and I'm going, so there's no sense in you trying to argue me out of it." I headed for the door. "Ella. Jennie. Want to help me pack?"

My little sisters raced after me as I stamped up the stairs, leaving my sister and my aunt to mull over their misgivings without my presence.

2) WHAT LUCY DOESN'T REMEMBER

Cordelia

Aunt Hannah and I exchanged concerned glances as my little sisters left the room. Lucy's dream had come true. Hiram, her pa, wanted her to come home. Hiram was my stepfather, the meanest man I'd ever known. He'd treated me like dirt and worse, and he hadn't been much nicer to his own flesh-and-blood daughters. Why didn't Lucy remember the countless times he'd yelled at Ma, ranting about how all the boy babies except Ambrose had been miscarried or died at birth or shortly after? Over and over, he'd complained he was cursed with girls when he needed sons. What good were daughters who couldn't carry on his last name?

In spite of all the negative things Lucy must have heard come out of his mouth, she still believed her pa loved her. She blamed me for Ma dying because I ran away to get Aunt Hannah's help and left Lucy to care for the family. That is what she'd been referring to when she'd said, "I'm not a last-minute person. I plan what I do." I was spur-of-the-moment to her. It wouldn't do any good to tell her I'd agonized over whether to run away for a month before I actually did it, and I wouldn't have gone at all except for the lecherous looks Hiram began giving me—but I'd never told her about those. She wouldn't have believed me anyway.

I sighed. "Why doesn't she remember what Hiram is really like, how he considers daughters worthless?"

"I don't know," Aunt Hannah said, "but there's nothing we can

4

say that will change her mind." She crossed to the window and stared out at the busy street as though she might find answers there. "If we try to tell her what to expect, she'll just say we're meddling and be angry with us. We can't keep her from going, but I don't want her traveling alone. She's only thirteen." Her lips formed a tight smile. "I suppose I'm being overprotective. You made the trip alone at that age. I guess I'll have to leave the hotel in your hands and take her."

On impulse, I said, "I can go instead."

"You? Why would you want to go anywhere near Hiram after the way he treated you?"

"Ever since Mr. O'Rourke came through last week with news of my father maybe being out by Pikes Peak looking for gold, I've thought of trying to find him. I keep going back and forth between yes and no, but I need to find out if he ever realized I existed, and if he did, why he didn't try to see me. I'm being stupid, but I—"

She stepped away from the window and put a hand on my shoulder. "It's not stupid to wonder, Cordelia."

"All this talk about my sisters' father wanting them, even when I'm certain it's not because he really cares for them, makes me want to learn more about mine." I bit my lip. "The stage that stops in Hidden Springs leaves immediately for Junction City and meets up with the new Pikes Peak Express that goes on to Denver City. I wouldn't have to see Hiram at all—or at least not for more than a few minutes—if he meets the stage—and he probably won't."

"How do you know so much about the stage routes?"

"I checked after Mr. O'Rourke said my father might be in the Denver area. Then I decided I wouldn't go. But now, with Lucy needing a chaperone, well, it seems like the right thing to do." I sighed. "I'd best go talk to her and try to make peace or it will be a long stage ride."

"Good luck," Aunt Hannah called after me as I left the lobby.

When I reached Lucy's room, the door was open. She was tossing dresses onto the foot of her bed. Ella and Jennie were perched at the head, each with a pillow wrapped in her arms.

Ella pointed to a blue calico. "Take that one. You look so pretty in it."

Jennie asked, "How long before we can come?"

Lucy folded the blue dress neatly. "I don't know. I'll ask Pa when I get there."

I knocked on the open door. "Lucy, may I come in?"

Her back stiffened. "I told you I'm going. There's nothing you can say to stop me."

She had not invited me in, so I stayed put. "I just came to tell you Aunt Hannah doesn't want you traveling alone, so I'm escorting you to Hidden Springs."

She whirled to face me. "Why? What trouble do you plan to cause?"

"No trouble. I won't even see your pa or Ambrose unless they meet the stage. I will be continuing on to Denver City."

She flounced to the dresser and removed another frock from the drawer. "Denver City? What's there?" She held the dress in front of her, shaking out the folds, pressing it to her and looking in the mirror before laying it on the bed.

"I have business there."

She faced me again, her eyes narrowing. "I don't suppose you're going to tell me what your business is?"

"I'm not."

"So why are you here?"

I sighed. I was no good at peacemaking. "Only to tell you we'll be traveling together."

She straightened, and her chin came up. "Well, now I know."

Amazing how a younger sister can dismiss an older one.

3) WHAT SHE KNEW

Lucy

I folded the green, linsey-woolsey frock I had chosen for wearing around the house to do chores in and added it to the pile of clothing to take to Hidden Springs, my mind on Cordelia and the way she was always badmouthing Pa. She hated him so much she probably considered his wanting me home the worst news she'd had in a long time.

When Cordelia had run away, Ma got even sicker than she already was, worrying about her safety and about who would take care of the family with Cordelia gone. I did my best, but I didn't even know how to make bread, so Ma couldn't stay in bed like Doc Sloan said she should. Instead, she shuffled to the rocker and guided me through each step. I was too small to take over Cordelia's laundry job with Mrs. Collins at the boarding house, so we didn't have that money. Plus, I couldn't keep up with all the home laundry and gardening chores. Jennie had been three and Ella five, young enough I had to watch out for them besides doing all my chores.

Then Pa got beat up by the slave hunters, his ribs broken and his chest branded with a horseshoe. After that, Ambrose taught me to milk the cow so he could work more hours at the blacksmith shop.

Getting to know Ambrose better was the only good part about Cordelia being gone. She always said Ambrose was Pa's favorite because he was a boy, and Pa didn't like us because we were girls. Pa sometimes said mean things, mostly to Cordelia because she wasn't his. We never told anyone outside the family, but at home, we all knew.

I used to look up to my sister. That was when we all called her Delia. I thought she was strong and smart and good. I thought she loved us. But I found out she was jealous. She didn't have a father, and we did. When she ran away, I had my first chance to spend time with my brother alone and find out he wasn't the stuck-up, better-than-the-rest-of-you person she always said he was.

"Lucy." Ella tugged my sleeve. "I'm talking to you, Lucy."

I straightened and blinked. "I'm sorry. I was thinking."

"About what?" Jennie asked.

"About the stone house Ambrose built. I finally get to see what it looks like. And when I show Pa how good I am at keeping house, he's going to send for you, and we'll all be together again."

"Except for Cordelia." Ella's forehead wrinkled. "Why's she taking you home when she doesn't want you to go? And why's she going to Denver City?"

"She's not telling," I said.

But I knew.

Aunt Hannah's friend, Mr. O'Rourke, a traveling photographer, had come through a week or so ago and said someone named Miz Wilma had told him Justin Quinn, Cordelia's real father, might be somewhere near Pikes Peak panning for gold. She hadn't gone to look for him then, but she was now. She was jealous because I had a father who wanted me and she didn't.

***

The next afternoon, clutching my borrowed copy of *Godey's Lady's Book*, I stood outside a small room at the back of the church where the women's Bible study group met, waiting for the meeting to break up so I could return the magazine and tell my aunts that Pa had sent for me. Aunt Hilda was the minister's wife, so she led the study. Aunt May attended because she was the banker's wife; supporting the church was expected of someone with her position in society.

Physically, my aunts had a strong family resemblance. May, Hilda, and Hannah were all tall blondes with blue eyes. It was their petticoats that set them apart. Aunt Hannah never wore more than four, and her skirts hung embarrassingly straight. Aunt Hilda usually donned six for an acceptable fullness. Aunt May dressed in nine petticoats that rustled and held out her skirts in a fashionable, almost

8

perfect, bell shape, befitting her social position.

At four o'clock, Aunt Hilda led a prayer to close the meeting. After the "amen," women began drifting toward the door, chatting on their way. I got my first clear view of Aunt May's new gown as she stood to leave. The dress had no collar, leaving Aunt May's entire neck exposed, and her skirt was a perfect bell, indicating that she had received the cage crinoline advertised in the issue of *Godey's* I held in my hand. Aunt Hilda's face held a sour look, and I wondered if Aunt May's choice of neckline for church wear caused it.

Aunt May nodded at Aunt Hilda and came toward the door, so I moved out of the corner. "Aunt May."

"Lucy, what are you doing here?"

"I came to tell you and Aunt Hilda my news." I peeked around Aunt May's shoulder to see Aunt Hilda accompanying Mrs. Baxter to the door. Both women seemed surprised to see me.

Mrs. Baxter nodded and left.

Aunt Hilda tilted her head. "What is it, Lucy?"

"Can we sit?" I pointed at the recently vacated chairs.

"Of course," Aunt Hilda said.

She stepped back into the room, and I followed with Aunt May. When we were seated, I pulled Ambrose's letter from my pocket. "I'm going home."

Aunt May snatched the paper from my hand and unfolded it. After a quick scan of the contents, she said, "Finally, your father has gotten some sense. It's about time he got you away from Hannah's influence with all her suffragette talk."

"She doesn't want me to go," I said.

Aunt Hilda, her mouth pursed, grabbed the letter from Aunt May, clearly aggravated that Aunt May had read it first. Aunt Hilda put on the spectacles that hung from a chain around her neck and began reading. When she finished, she folded the letter and handed it to me.

"Regardless of what Hannah wants or says, she has no right to keep you from your father. Remember, the Bible commands you to honor your father and mother."

"Exactly," I agreed. "That's why I'm here. I came to tell you I'm leaving on tomorrow's stage. Cordelia is accompanying me to Hidden Springs."

Both of my aunts scowled. While they disagreed on many things, their contempt for Cordelia was not one of them.

"Watch out for that one," Aunt May said.

***

The next morning, Aunts Hilda and May stood with me and my little sisters on the wood plank walk in front of the stage station. Aunt Hannah and Cordelia huddled off to one side, whispering, probably badmouthing my pa like they always did.

Aunt Hilda threw them a frown. "Never mind their nonsense," she said. "Your pa needs you."

Jennie and Ella wrapped their arms around me. Jennie tilted her head back and looked up, brown eyes sad. "We want to go, too. We miss Ambrose. He used to play with us."

I wondered how much they remembered about our family in Hidden Springs. I touched the locket I wore, the one containing a few strands of Ma's hair. Aunt Hannah had bought each of us girls one, saying the snippets of Ma's hair would keep her close to us. But she hadn't given us anything to keep Pa or Ambrose close. Instead, she'd whisked us girls away as soon as Ma's funeral was over with barely a chance to say goodbye. I had thought we were visiting for a few weeks, maybe until Pa's ribs and the burn he'd gotten from being beaten by the border ruffians had healed. But Aunt Hannah had meant to keep us forever—or at least until Pa got around to asking for us.

Now he wanted me, and Aunt Hannah thought I shouldn't go. But he was my pa, so I didn't have a choice. Even if I'd had one, I'd still want a home with Pa over life with my aunts in Westport.

The stagecoach rattled down the street and came to a stop.

"Time to leave," Aunt May said. "You'll write, of course." She hugged me. "Have a good trip."

"Goodbye, Lucy," Ella said, tears in her eyes.

I received a quick embrace from Aunt Hilda and then bent to hug each of my little sisters. "Goodbye." It was hard to keep from tearing up. I couldn't imagine a reason to return to Westport, so I wouldn't see them again until they came to live in Hidden Springs, something I knew Aunt Hannah would try to prevent.

Aunt Hannah came to say goodbye then, enfolding me in her arms and pressing her lips next to my ear. "If life with your father doesn't work out the way you imagine, you can always come back."

"Thank you," I said, rigid in her arms.

Cordelia and I climbed into the coach. A man and a woman occupied the bench seat at the other end, and neither my sister nor I wanted the center seat, so we sat beside each other. The driver cracked his whip and yelled for the horses to get going.

Cordelia leaned in and whispered, "Your pa's not the person you think he is."

I boiled over, snapping at her. "What do you know about fathers? Why don't you want me to be with mine when you're going off to find a man you've never met, who never even wanted you?" I looked up and met our travelling companions' widened eyes.

Cordelia's cheeks flushed. She wanted to tell me off, but unlike me, she had good manners. She turned her face to the window, so all I could see was the back of her bonnet, shutting me out the way she did whenever I said something she didn't like.

Realizing I'd made our travelling companions uncomfortable, I gazed out my own window, imagining what Cordelia would have said if she'd been rude enough to tell me what she thought in front of strangers. She'd say, "Remember how Hiram didn't even look at you girls when you said goodbye to him. He didn't care that his daughters were leaving because he still had Ambrose, his only son, the only child who mattered to him."

She was right about what happened, but not about why. I'd played that scene over in my mind hundreds of times. Pa had just buried Ma and yet another baby. He was in pain from broken ribs and a horrible burn. He'd agreed we should go with Aunt Hannah before Ma died, and he was too full of grief to stop her from taking us.

I closed my eyes and imagined my homecoming. Ambrose would come for me in a wagon and drive me to our new house where Pa would be waiting. His face would light up in a big smile when he saw me, and he'd say how grown up I was and how glad he was to have me home where I belonged. I'd fix us a meal of ham and mashed potatoes and peas, and he'd say I'd become a fine cook and some man would be lucky to marry me someday. I was almost glad my little sisters hadn't come with me. For a little while, I could shine as the only daughter in Pa's house.

4) CLOSE QUARTERS

Cordelia

We spent the night in Lawrence and were up early to board the stage to Topeka. Lucy was still mad at me. Thankfully, Lawrence had been the destination of the passengers she had blurted out my business in front of, so I didn't have to stare across the coach at them. We arrived at the stage and boarded first. Soon, two miners in a rush to the gold fields and a priest on his way to St. Marys joined us.

The miners clearly considered themselves men although they were boys about my age—somewhere between sixteen and twenty— old enough to shave although they hadn't, leaving a rough smattering of short stubble on their chins. The odor of last night's whisky and stale perfume lingered on them.

The first one in lit up at the sight of Lucy and shoved himself onto the bench beside her, squeezing into the small space, his legs brushing hers and his buttocks shoving her over as he settled in.

I leaned forward, looked straight at him, and gave him my best glare, wanting to tell him Lucy was only thirteen, and he needed to leave children alone. I held my tongue because I knew what Lucy's reaction would be. She thought that because she was a head taller than I, with a full head of shiny black hair and bosoms that strained against the bodice of her dress, she was an adult and had some sense.

The other man frowned as he entered and saw no more room on our bench for him. He settled on the middle seat opposite his companion. The somewhat rotund priest behind him settled on the back seat and folded his arms across his chest, his stomach providing a resting place for his ample arms. He fixed disapproving gray eyes on the man beside Lucy, who still shifted in his seat, ostensibly looking for a comfortable position but actually taking advantage of the excuse to bump against Lucy's loins.

"'Scuse me," the squirmer mumbled. He bent forward, looking around Lucy to me. "Would you mind moving down aways?"

Lucy shot me a sideways glance. I thought seriously of moving to the middle seat, but there was nothing but a strap to hold onto to keep me from flying into someone's lap, something I found repulsive, so I scooted another inch and pressed against my side of the coach. Lucy smashed up against me.

The brazen young man smiled, leaned against the back wall of the coach, and flung an arm behind Lucy. "There now," he said, "it's right comfy. Don't you think so, Miss——?"

"Miss Pierce," Lucy replied.

He flashed another smile and blinked his long-lashed blue eyes at her. "Bob Sims." He stuck out his hand, taking hers up right out of her lap. "Pleased to meet you."

Lucy looked startled, but she didn't pull away.

Bob must have felt encouraged when she didn't jerk her hand back. "We're going all the way to Pikes Peak and the gold fields. My pa's already staked a claim and bringing in fifty or sixty dollars a day, sometimes more."

The other man frowned. "We're not supposed to be spreading that news around, Bob."

"Damn it, Scott, you're just jealous because I'm sitting over here by the pretty one." He glanced at the priest. "'Scuse me, Father."

The priest's eyes hooded. "You are not excused until you show proper respect to these young ladies. Let go of the girl's hand and behave properly in the company of women."

Bob release Lucy's hand. "Never meant to offend, Father." He moved to his side of the coach as far as the small seat would allow.

At that moment, the driver cracked the whip, and the horses took off, leaving all of us bouncing up and thumping down on our bottoms.

We were off.

5) A SOUR SISTER

Lucy

Between the priest and Cordelia, it was going to be a boring trip. Of course, I couldn't blame the priest; he was just doing what priests do. But Cordelia sat there all sour and hateful. No wonder. Bob and Scott had made it clear they thought I was the prettier one. When Cordelia had run away four years ago, she had passed for a boy. She still could. She had practically no bosoms at all.

I could have had a beau by now if my aunts weren't so strict. Me being too young to keep company with someone was the only thing they agreed on. As for Cordelia, she would probably end up an old maid like Aunt Hannah. Both of them saw men as the enemy and went to all those suffragette meetings, messing in politics, something both Aunt May and Aunt Hilda said was unladylike and beyond a woman's sphere.

Beside me, Bob's leg slid over and touched mine. I shifted away as much as I could, glad the six petticoats I wore put some distance between our limbs. I had wanted to wear nine like Aunt May, but Cordelia and Aunt Hannah objected, saying space in a stagecoach was limited.

"So where are you ladies headed?" Bob asked.

"Hidden Springs," I answered. "But Cordelia's going on to Denver City."

Cordelia elbowed my ribs.

Scott's eyebrows shot up. "What's in Denver City?"

"A sick friend," Cordelia said.

"Really?" I asked, the story being new to me. "Who?"

She crossed her arms and stiffened her back. "Miz Wilma, if you must know. She's laid up with a broken leg."

The coach hit a bump. Bob fell against me, then brushed a hand across my waist as he straightened. "And Hidden Springs? What's there?"

"Her father," Cordelia snapped. "A big, burly blacksmith who will break you in half if you dare come near his daughter. He expects her to marry well, and your life is in danger if you do anything to jeopardize that."

"Cordelia," I said, "that's the first good word you've had to say about Pa."

She looked at me, frowned, and showed me the back of her bonnet again.

***

It was late afternoon when we reached Topeka.

The driver opened the stage door, helped us down, and pointed to a hotel across the street. "Best place for a room if you want one. We'll be leaving out of here for Junction City at three in the morning. Don't be late. We got a schedule to keep. We won't wait."

Cordelia eyed our two heavy trunks stowed on top of the stage. "Will our trunks be safe if we leave them where they are? We have our necessaries in my bag."

"Yes, but like I said, three in the morning."

"We'll be here," she replied.

I followed Cordelia to the hotel. After securing accommodations, we went to the dining room for a meal of beef stew and biscuits. After our meal, Cordelia left word at the desk to rouse us at two o'clock, so we could prepare to meet the stage.

Once in our room, my sister laid aside her bonnet and loosened the bodice of her dress. "You shouldn't be leading on men like those two miners."

"What's the harm in a little flirting? I'm getting off the stage tomorrow."

"That's nice for you, but I may have to put up with them all the way to Denver City, and your actions have led them to think they can be familiar."

Exasperated, I took off all my petticoats and draped them over a chair back. "As sour as you've been, I can't imagine anyone even speaking to you."

She rolled her eyes. Wearing our chemises for nightdresses, we got into bed, turned our backs to each other, and didn't say another word.

6) MEMORIES OF A RUNAWAY

Cordelia

I was awakened at two o'clock by a knock on the door as I had requested. It took some nudging before Lucy finally stumbled to her feet, splashed water on her face, and arranged her hair. By that time, I was tapping my foot, ready to leave.

We boarded the stage to find the two would-be miners had not arrived. When they didn't show up by three, the driver left without them, just as he had promised, so this part of the trip included me, Lucy, and the priest.

It wasn't long before we were coming to St. Marys mission, and memories overwhelmed me. Miz Wilma, who had come to take two Indian orphans to their tribe, had let me off at the wharf here. It was where I first met Mr. O'Rourke and learned to take daguerreotypes.

The stage stopped long enough to let the priest out and for us to eat a midday meal before quickly returning to the road.

With only Lucy and me aboard, we bounced along, side by side, not looking at each other, watching the scenery our only pastime. Four years ago, it had taken me two weeks to make the trip we would make now in two and a half days. We passed Odgen, a land office city, and then the remains of Pawnee were in sight. Everything except for the stone territorial legislature building had been destroyed by the soldiers on orders from Washington. There was nothing left of Miss Millie's Eating House or Mr. Baldwin's livery stable, the place where Max kidnapped me after he killed a man for dishonoring his sister.

I hadn't thought of Max in a long time. Remembering how Aunt Hannah said I liked him, and how people who traveled the trail a lot crossed paths sometimes, I couldn't help wondering if I'd meet up with him on this trip.

7) HIDDEN SPRINGS AT LAST

Lucy

When we reached the Hidden Springs turnoff, home was only a mile away. I straightened in my seat, excited to see how the town had changed during my four-year absence. In his letters, Ambrose had said even with the Panic the last couple of years, the town and Pa's blacksmith shop had done well. All I knew about the Panic was what I heard lodgers at the hotel talking about: In 1857 a ship on the way from the San Francisco Mint to the east sank with thirty thousand pounds of gold. I couldn't even imagine what that much gold looked like. Aunt Hannah said banks were shutting down, railroads were going bankrupt, and farmers were getting less money for grain and not paying their mortgages. With fewer people heading west, fewer people stayed at the hotel. For most of last year, Aunt Hannah said the hotel barely made enough to stay open and that my pa and uncles complained they weren't seeing the profits they once did. Those hard times seemed to have gone by without touching Hidden Springs.

As the horses pulled the stage up the main street, I saw a general store alongside Mrs. Collins's boardinghouse. Pa's shop was across the street from the boardinghouse, and there was a new livery stable beside it. Ambrose had said the stable was Pa's, a good addition to his blacksmithing business. He said Pa made an agreement with other stable owners along the trail. Folks could rent a horse at one of the other towns and leave it with Ambrose if they weren't going back the way they'd come. Their owners would send someone to collect their animals or pay for Ambrose to return them. Mr. Clark was working with Pa at the shop, so Ambrose could take care of the stable and the farm chores. I hoped I remembered how to milk a cow like Ambrose had taught me because it sounded like Pa kept him awful busy.

Folks on the boardwalk lining the street turned to watch the stage pull up in front of the boarding house.

The driver opened the door. "Which trunk belongs to the young lady getting off here?"

"The larger one," I said.

He set a wooden step on the ground and took my hand to balance me as I descended from the coach.

I turned to watch the driver and a helper bring down my trunk. Cordelia leaned forward from inside the coach. "I hope everything goes the way you imagine it will," she said.

"Thank you," I replied, not believing her for a minute. She wanted to be right; in fact, she knew in her mind that she was right, so what really happened wouldn't matter. She'd just say it meant something different than what I saw and felt.

With my trunk on the walk, the driver and his helper talked with a new passenger while loading his trunk. All that time, I glanced up and down the street, shifting this way and that, looking first toward the blacksmith shop and then down the road that led to our homestead. I didn't expect to see Ambrose or Pa coming from the direction of our home, but where were they? It looked as though I would have to leave my trunk on the street, something I didn't want to do, while I went to the shop to get help with it.

"Lucy!"

The shout came from behind me. I turned to see a tall, young man waving at me. His black hair grazed his shoulders and lifted in the breeze. He called my name again and trotted toward me. It was Ambrose. I had not recognized my own brother.

"Ambrose." I dashed off the boardwalk toward him. We met in the middle of the street, laughing and hugging each other before dodging an oncoming wagon.

When we were safely on the walk in front of Mrs. Collins's boardinghouse, he held me at arm's length. "You've grown," he said.

"So have you. So much I didn't recognize you."

Ambrose had always been big for his age. Fourteen now, he had probably gotten his full height. He was thin but muscular. He looked like a younger version of our father. I figured that pleased Pa.

"I wasn't sure you'd be on this stage, and I didn't want to block the stop with our wagon. Stay here, and I'll be right back."

"Where's Pa?" I asked.

"He's finishing a new job. You know Pa. He always finishes on time."

"Sure," I said to his back as he dashed across the street toward the stable. The stage took off, and I sat on my trunk, waiting, wishing for the homecoming I'd pictured, telling myself I shouldn't be disappointed. After all, I knew work came first with Pa. Still, it had been four years.

"Lucy! My word! Is that you, girl?"

I stood and spun around. "Mrs. Collins. Yes, it is."

Smoothing her hands on her apron, she stepped out of the doorway of the boarding house, a welcoming smile on her face. "Hiram mentioned he'd sent for you. I'm betting he'll be running off all the young men in town because he's set on finding you a proper match. He has high hopes you'll marry well."

"I know." I understood she meant Pa was proud of me and wanted me to have a good life. But I was only thirteen and wanted some time at home first—and a say in picking my life partner.

She took my hands in hers and gave them a squeeze. "How are your sisters?"

"Ella and Jennie are well, but they were disappointed they couldn't come. I told them it wouldn't be long, that I'd show Pa real quick I could take care of my chores and them, too."

She let go my hands. "And Cordelia?"

Some of the joy left me. "You just missed her. She came with me on the stage to see I got home okay, and she went on to catch the Express to Denver City."

"Denver City? Why is she going there?"

I had to think fast. I couldn't say she went to look for her real pa because Mrs. Collins thought my pa was hers.

"She went to pan for gold," I said.

"Alone? I can't believe Hiram would allow that."

"I guess he thinks she's a lost cause, that Aunt Hannah's opinions have rubbed off on her. She believes a woman can do anything a man can do, so she's bound to get rich prospecting for gold."

Mrs. Collins shook her head. "She has always been independent, taking off like she did when your Ma was sick."

A wagon creaked up beside us, and Ambrose called out, "Whoa." He set the brake and hopped down. "Hello, Mrs. Collins. I see you managed to recognize our Lucy."

"It did take a moment. She surely has grown into a fine young lady."

I ducked my head, my face warming at the compliment.

"Yes, ma'am," Ambrose said, hefting my trunk and stowing it on the back of the wagon. "You ready, Lucy?"

"I am." I gathered my skirts, and Ambrose steadied me as I climbed onto the seat. "Goodbye, Mrs. Collins."

"Goodbye, dear."

Ambrose drove the mules past the two blocks of businesses, heading toward our place. In the second block was the church and a school.

"Ma would have given anything if we'd had a school to go to," I said.

"We have a building, but we need a teacher. Ours got married as soon as school let out this spring."

"Do you think the town council will find someone by fall, so when Ella and Jennie come, they can go to school?"

"They won't be coming for a while."

"By fall when school starts, don't you think?"

"Maybe. Depends on Pa."

"Well, I know that, but you said in your letter they could come if I showed I could handle the chores with time left over. Besides, they're nine and seven now. They don't need looking after every minute."

When Ambrose didn't say anything, I figured he didn't have any more opinions on the matter. We rode in silence past several new cabins spread out along the road at the edge of town.

Ambrose nodded at a sturdy-looking log home. "That's the last one until we get to our house."

Less than five minutes later, we passed a stand of trees. "There it is," he said.

Even though Ambrose had described the house in his letters—a two-story limestone with four bedrooms—I marveled at the size. "You built that?"

Ambrose grinned as he guided the mules down a circular drive and stopped in front of the stone steps that led to a large wooden door.

He leapt off the wagon and came around to help me down. His hand on my back, he guided me to the door while telling me the details involved in building the house. "I was apprenticed for two years with a stone-cutter who taught me to both cut the stones and lay them. My work paid for the limestone."

I smiled at his pride in the house he had helped build with his own hands, and, as our father's only son, would someday inherit. Just the thought of cutting, hauling, and building the walls for a house this size amazed me. With his knowledge of blacksmithing and stone masonry, he had the skills to go far in the world. Some lucky girl would have a prosperous husband in him. I swallowed hard. There I was, thinking of him getting married and having a family and how successful he would be—exactly the kind of thing I had been frowning on others doing about me.

Ambrose reached for the iron doorknob beside the large knocker and opened the door. "Ladies first." He ushered me inside. "Have a look around while I get your trunk."

The entrance hall was large with a stairway to the right. A hallway extended the length of the house with doors to rooms on either side. I stepped to the first door on the left and opened it. The room was large and empty of furniture except for Ma's old rocker. A fireplace took up a good portion of one wall.

The sound of the front door closing caused me to step back into the hall. Ambrose stood holding my trunk. "Come on. I'll show you to your room."

He took the stairs ahead of me, handling the heavy trunk as though it were nothing, but I supposed that someone who lifted rocks into place found a chest of clothes and keepsakes a light load.

The upstairs, like the main floor, was divided by a hall. My room was at the back.

"Get the door, Lucy. My hands are full."

"Sorry, I was taking everything in." I opened the door.

Ambrose went in and set the trunk on a chest at the end of the double bed. Besides the chest, there was a dresser with a mirror on one wall. Light streamed through a window. Curious about the view, I went to look out. The sight of our old cabin brought tears to my eyes. I remembered our last night and day in that tiny home, the whole cabin scarcely bigger than the room I was now to call my own, the first such room I'd ever had. In Westport, I shared with Ella and Jennie, preferring three to a room to sharing with Cordelia.

Ambrose stood behind me and placed his hand on my shoulder. "Are you okay?"

I shivered and wiped away a stray tear. "Just seeing our old home made me think of Ma dying and Aunt Hannah stealing us girls."

Ambrose stepped back and turned me to face him. He held me at arm's length. "Stealing you? What do you mean?"

I let out an exasperated breath. "They'd barely filled in Ma's grave when Aunt Hannah and Cordelia rushed us out the door with less than a minute to say goodbye." My voice cracked, and I swallowed hard. "I thought we'd come back as soon as Pa's ribs healed, but every time I asked, they put me off with 'Someday. We don't know when.' They never meant for me to come home."

"But Pa agreed you should go. I heard him. And Ma agreed. She wanted you to sleep with her that night so she could say goodbye."

"But she didn't know she was going to die." My voice cracked, and I pulled away from his grasp. "She'd never have said we should go if she had known what would happen. She'd have wanted me to stay and take care of you and Pa."

Ambrose shook his head. "It was too much for you. You were only nine. She wanted you to have some good times before taking over a house and family. Cordelia was planning to stay and care for Ma."

I whirled around and paced the floor. "Well, she didn't stay and take care of anyone, did she? She got away as fast as she could without even a thought to you."

"She knew Pa would never let me go with you. Besides, I had to take care of him until his ribs and burn healed."

I clenched my fists at my side. "Why are you sticking up for her? If she hadn't run away and caused Ma all that worry, Ma might still be alive."

"You got that right," Pa said.

Ambrose and I turned to see him standing in the doorway.

Pa crossed to the window and looked out at the cabin. "Hadn't of been for Cordelia, you might have had your Ma enjoying this new house and a little brother running around instead of the two of them buried in the cemetery."

24

Finally, someone who agreed with me.

Ambrose stepped aside. "I got the mules and wagon to put away. I'm sure you two have some catching up to do."

Pa put his hand on my shoulder, and we stood staring down at the old cabin for a few seconds longer. I took a deep breath, inhaling the smells of sweat and smoke that clung to his clothes. Eyes closed, I felt the connection I always sought and so often escaped me.

Pa cleared his throat. "You need anything else in this room? Mrs. Collins helped fix it up."

I glanced around. The bed was made up with a quilt. I crossed to the dresser and pulled out a drawer. It was deep and wide, large enough to hold my frocks. "Everything's perfect."

"Remember to thank her at supper tonight."

My stomach did a flip. "Supper? She's coming here tonight?" I hadn't even seen the stove, let alone figured out how to cook on it. There was a stove, wasn't there? A big house like this must have more than a fireplace for cooking.

"She invited us to supper at the boardinghouse. Special for your homecoming."

"Oh." I let out a breath, then hoped I didn't sound as relieved as I felt. "Yes, I'll be sure to thank her."

"Let's have a look around then, so you can get unpacked and get to work on your chores. I need to get back to the shop."

Chores? I had just arrived. I was exhausted from the bouncing stage. Now there were chores.

Pa was already in the hall, pointing out rooms. "There's Ambrose's room and there's mine and there's the spare." He moved to the stairway and descended, talking all the while. "We haven't furnished much of the downstairs yet. Thought I'd leave that to you. There's a stack of catalogues from back east in the parlor. Course, I have a few ideas on that, too, and Ambrose is a good cabinet-maker, so there's no need to order something unless it's top notch."

"What about Ella and Jennie?" I asked

We reached the bottom of the stairs, and he headed down the hall.

He stopped and looked at me, forehead furrowing. "What about them?"

"When they come? Will they get the spare room or will they move in with me?"

"Never thought that far ahead. Probably with you. After all, a spare room is just that. Spare."

"Of course." Disappointed, I followed him into the kitchen. An iron cook stove sat to one side of the room with a work table and pie safe. Cast iron skillets and pots hung from pegs on the wall. Across the room by the window were an oak table and chairs for meals.

Pa opened a pie safe door. "Plenty of storage room here, plus there's a root cellar out back." He pointed to a paper on the work table. "I made up a list of your chores. Figured with you living in a city, you probably forgot what needs done on a farm. Well, I got to be going. Have a look in the other rooms. Not much to see, but the parlor has your ma's old rocker, and the dining room has that buffet we brought from Westport. The library doesn't have many books yet, but I set up my desk in there." He stood, looking at the floor as though he were trying to figure out if he'd forgotten anything. "That's it, I guess. I'll send Ambrose to pick you up for supper."

"Thanks, Pa."

I watched him leave, my heart heavy. I had pictured a hug for my homecoming, or at least a hello. I had gotten neither. But I was home, and already I had a list of chores to do.

I picked up the list and carried it to the dining table by the window. My work was spelled out in a careful, even hand.

fix meals
clean up after meals
gather eggs
feed chickens
feed the pigs
milk cow morning and evening and let out to pasture and bring in
weed the garden
bake
do laundry

The list went on. I put it down and looked around the kitchen. The first thing was to get acquainted with the stove. I opened a door and peeked into its dark interior. There were ashes. Beside the stove, I spied a bucket with ash clinging to its side. Now I knew what to use to empty the stove before starting a new fire. But where to dump the ashes?

I went out the back door and wandered about, to the chicken house, to the barn, and finally, to the place calling me since I had seen it through my bedroom window—our old cabin, my home for less than a year, the place where my mother died in labor that produced a stillborn son.

I opened the door to the cabin and was struck by the emptiness. The only furniture remaining, two benches and a wood plank table where, four years ago when I was nine, we ate our meals near the fireplace. Ambrose's bed, Ma's rocker, the straw pallet in the corner my sisters and I had slept on, the buffet that had divided my parents' bed from the rest of the house were all gone. My eyes flicked across that barren space to where Ma had last lain in bed, our stillborn brother in her arms, pale, unmoving, empty of life and spirit. Ambrose had stood beside me, his arm around my shoulders, his breathing shallow and rough, his chest muscles jerking, barely holding in his emotions, my big brother being strong for me as we said goodbye to Ma.

A faint light filtered through the small window she had looked out of so many times during her sickness. Shadows flickered across the room as tree limbs swayed in the breeze, mesmerizing me, drawing me across the room to the spot where her bed had been. I sank to my knees and into the past, to that last night when we girls slept with her, Ella and Jennie at the other end of the bed, going to sleep giggling and singing their ABCs, and me snuggled next to Ma as she painted pretty word pictures of us girls visiting Aunt Hannah and going to school and making friends and sleeping in her old bedroom. Sometime during those visions of good times I drifted off in Ma's arms.

I woke up to her screams.

"Get Hannah. Get Hannah." She clutched her stomach. "Oh, no! No!"

And then Aunt Hannah was there, shooing me and Jennie and Ella out of the room, sending Ambrose for Doc Sloan. Then the waiting, and Pa ranting about Aunt Hannah and Cordelia keeping Ma from her bed while they washed clothes the day before, causing the loss of his son. And at the end, Doc Sloan saying, "She's gone."

My hand closed around the locket with her hair inside. I squeezed my eyes shut and knelt there for a long time, flashes of memories, good and bad, tearing my heart, aching for our family, for my mother, for her smile, for the sweet cornbread she made that was like no one else's. I ached for the feel of her pulling a brush through my hair. "A hundred strokes a day," she always said, "will keep your hair healthy and shiny." I could almost feel her hands stroking my hair.

Opening my eyes, I stared at a place where the wall met the floorboards, at a crack, at something in the crack. I bent forward on hands and knees and crept a foot or so, reached for the thin object, curved and smooth on one side, rough on the other. I pulled it out of the crack and held it to the light, breathing in my surprise and amazement. It was Ma's comb, the one we thought lost forever after the slave hunters had torn our cabin apart. Holding the mantilla-shaped brown and gold faux tortoise shell comb, I saw that one tooth had been broken but the tiny stones of the pique work design were all present. The comb had been lost for four years. Finding it after so long was like Ma's spirit had guided me to it. I pressed it to my chest and closed my eyes, holding on to that feeling of closeness.

"Lucy, are you in here?"

My eyelids blinked open. I slid the comb in my pocket. I wasn't ready to share it, not even with my brother.

Ambrose stood in the doorway. Seeing me, he crossed the room and squatted beside me. "Something about the way you looked at the cabin earlier made me think you'd be here." He stood and held out his hand. "Come on. You have chores before we go to Mrs. Collins' place for supper."

"Yes, chores," I said, taking his hand and letting him steady me as I rose to my feet. I glanced around the cabin, vacant except for my memories and the old table and bench seats by the fireplace. "I lived most of my life in Westport, but this was my first real home, my only real home. Oh, Ambrose, the new house is wonderful, but it's so empty."

"Not for long, Lucy. You'll fill it with furniture and memories."

"I wonder how long that will take."

"That depends on when you start. How about now?"

"I suppose. What's first?"

"I taught you to milk a cow. Let's find out what you remember about that."

I groaned and laughed and followed him to the barn.

28

8) UNWELCOME ATTENTION

Cordelia

While the driver unloaded Lucy's trunk and the mail pouches, a man approached him and pointed to bags stacked by a bench on the boardwalk.

I leaned against the side of the coach and looked out at Lucy standing in front of Mrs. Collins's boardinghouse, anxiously glancing this way and that, looking for Hiram. Poor girl. She'd really expected her father to show up.

"Lucy," someone called. A tall young man dashed into the street, and I realized it was Ambrose.

Lucy ran toward him, and he pulled her into his arms for a welcoming hug. The pure joy on his face brought back the memory of Aunt Hannah driving us girls out of town while Ambrose stood waving, sad and alone.

Whatever had happened after that day, he had gotten through it. He looked tall and strong and even happy. He seemed to have done better than we girls. Had Aunt Hannah and I been wrong to take my sisters with us? More and more I asked myself that.

The stage door opened, and the man who had been talking with the driver stepped in and took the seat across from me at the other end of the coach. He was perhaps twenty, of medium height, neatly dressed in brown trousers, a brown plaid shirt and a slouch hat. His boots were worn but polished and free of mud. From what I could see of his hair, it was also brown. He was clean shaven. He tipped his hat. "Miss," he said, glancing about as though he expected to see someone else in the coach.

I nodded and gave a lukewarm smile as a greeting. A woman alone, I did not want to encourage conversation with strangers.

"Martin Sims," he said. "On my way to Denver City."

"Cordelia Pierce," I said to be polite, but my neck muscles tightened. Sims was the last name of the two we'd left in Topeka. If this one was related to that pair, I definitely wanted nothing to do with him.

"You're related to the blacksmith then?" he asked. "Shouldn't you be getting off here?"

"I am related," I said, hating the lie but bound to it for Ma's memory's sake. I didn't want anyone to know her shame and stain her reputation. "I accompanied my sister Lucy home, but I, too, am bound for Denver City. An old friend has been injured, and I'm on my way to care for her until she gets on her feet."

Martin Sims seemed a serious young man, so unlike the other two that the last name might be a coincidence. "And you," I said, making polite conversation—after all, he had decent manners and we were going to be traveling together for some days. "What takes you to Denver City? Will you be prospecting for gold?"

"That was my intention. I have two partners, cousins, who were supposed to be on this stage."

"Oh," I said and sighed. So they were related.

He raised an eyebrow. "You've met them?"

"By them, I assume you mean Bob and Scott, two men who didn't make the stage in time and got left." I put a chill in my voice. "They attempted to become acquainted with my sister." Knowing the odious men were his relatives, I was ready to end our conversation.

"Bob must have taken the lead in that. He fancies himself attractive to ladies."

"Someone should tell him bad manners are not attractive."

His eyes twinkled, and he grinned. "Certainly, you must have done so."

The driver shouted and cracked his whip. I grasped the edge of the seat as the horses took off. Martin Sims clasped his hat and steadied himself. We jounced along, heading west toward Junction City.

Mr. Sims was not one to travel in silence. "So the young lady who disembarked in front of the station was also Miss Pierce."

"Yes."

"Your sister is a lovely young woman. You shouldn't fault my cousins for being attracted."

"She is a child of thirteen, too young for them. I brought that to their attention."

He looked surprised, but many people supposed Lucy to be older than I because of her well-developed bosom. In comparison, with a little chest binding, I should be able to pass for a boy forever.

"So you are the older sister?"

"I am."

"And protective, I see."

"Yes." What was wrong with this man that he couldn't see I was not interested in conversing with him?

Or maybe he did see. He looked out the coach window for all of three minutes before launching into another topic.

"Have you been to Denver City before?" he asked.

"No." I gazed at the passing landscape.

"But you have a friend there."

"My friend travels about the west helping people who have fallen ill. She is a healer."

"A woman, then?"

"Yes, Miz Wilma is a woman." I hoped the name would quiet him. He seemed suspicious that I had no friend and was going for some other purpose.

"An unmarried woman traveling alone."

"She is a widow."

"She is much older than you?"

"I should say. Perhaps as old as my grandmother." The thought stopped me. Miz Wilma and my grandmother were near the same age, about sixty, but Miz Wilma was strong whereas my grandmother spent her days in a dark room, grieving for her past with no outlook for the future.

"And traveling about the frontier alone?"

"You keep saying that as though she shouldn't be allowed to do so."

Another bump jostled us both. He reached for a handhold on his side.

"It's not that I don't think she should be allowed, only that it must be dangerous for a woman her age to be traveling alone."

"She's been doing it for years. She does not limit her good works to settlers but helps anyone or anything that needs it." I couldn't help smiling. "She even saved a skunk once. He was a companion in her wagon for a while."

"A skunk."

I laughed, remembering Stinky. "Sometimes a skunk is the only weapon needed to get rid of obnoxious people."

"Are you a suffragette, Miss Pierce?"

"I am. How observant of you to notice. What led you to think so?"

"Your rather abrupt manner with me and a general thorniness when what a woman may be allowed to do is brought up in casual conversation."

"Then, Mr. Sims, you must surely realize that I have no interest in talking with a man who believes women should get permission to lead their daily lives in any way they choose."

"When one has such a closed mind, Miss Pierce, she may fail to meet many people who might become friends."

I gave him what I hoped was a withering look before turning aside and watching the land pass in front of me.

***

We had barely pulled to a stop in Junction City when Bob and Scott came charging toward the coach, whooping as soon as Martin Sims disembarked, rushing up, slapping him on the back. "Thought we wouldn't catch up, did you?" Bob asked. "Thought you'd get all the gold for yourself?"

Scott looked around. "Tone it down, Bob. We don't want everyone knowing our business."

"Killjoy," Bob said.

Martin Sims saw to the transfer of all their baggage and had it stowed for loading onto the Express when it came through. I, too, had my trunk carried into the station for the same purpose. After leaving Junction City, we would sleep on the stage, the ground, or the floor of a station for at least the next ten nights as there were no more hotels on the route. I didn't look forward to that with three men—more counting the drivers. However, since a backup stage would travel with us to help us if wagon parts broke, our stage got stuck in the mud, or Indians or robbers attacked us, I hoped I might

32

be permitted to sleep in that coach or on the ground.

While the Sims boys traded stories, I got lodging at the nearest hotel. After requesting a knock on the door at five the next morning since the Pikes Peak Express stage would leave Junction City at six, I had a meal in the dining hall and went to my room.

The chamber was clean, and soon a knock came. A young boy about twelve was delivering a pitcher of water. He set it on the dresser next to a matching wash basin. I gave him a nickel for his trouble and thanked him. There was also a tin cup on the dresser, so I had a drink before I let down my hair and washed off the trail dust.

I went to sleep hoping for another passenger, someone who would dampen the miners' wild spirits, but with my luck, I'd probably get another one just like them.

9) WELCOME HOME

Lucy

I sat on the milking stool, squeezing Sunflower's teats, watching milk stream into the bucket. It was almost full, and she was almost empty. My hands ached. I hadn't done this job since Aunt Hannah had whisked me off to Westport.

Ambrose sat on a pile of hay beside me, giving advice from time to time and filling in between with stories about building the house and running a livery stable.

"Couple of fellows came in just after I got back to the stable from bringing you home. They wanted to make sure there was a place in Junction City to drop the horses they rented back in Topeka. The stage took off without them."

"Oh, did one man have dark-hair and blue eyes and the other have lighter brown hair and act more reserved?"

"Sort of. Was it your stage that left them?"

"Yes, they didn't show up on time." I squeezed the last drop out of Sunflower. "I'm done."

"Okay, we'll get the milk to the cellar and strain it into the milking pan to cool. I'll show you where."

He didn't offer to pick up the bucket, so I did. It was heavy. I had worked hard at the hotel, but I didn't often have to lift anything that weighed a lot. If I did, I didn't have to carry it very far. Now I walked a little lopsided as I followed my brother. Full milk pails were just the beginning of the heavy work I'd be doing here. I had to admit I hadn't thought of that during my daydreams of life at home.

After I took care of the milk, fed the chickens, and slopped the hogs, I left Ambrose chopping firewood while I hurried to my room to clean up for supper at the boardinghouse with Mrs. Collins.

An hour later, we were getting on the wagon when Ambrose asked, "Where was Cordelia going after you left the stage? How was she going to get back to Westport?"

"She wasn't going back. She was going to catch the Pikes Peak Express when she got to Junction City. She was on her way to Denver City to look for her father."

Ambrose perked up and started shooting questions at me. "Cordelia went looking for her father? Why did she think he was in Denver City? How does she even know who to look for?"

"Aunt Hannah knew him. And when Cordelia ran away that time, she met a traveling photographer and other people who travel back and forth on the trails. Anyway, they were on the lookout for him so they could tell Cordelia if they saw him."

"It sounds like she made some good friends." He laughed. "I suppose she'll have to put up with those would-be miners all the way to Denver City."

I rolled my eyes. "More likely, they'll have to put up with her. She's just like Aunt Hannah in her view of men. Absolutely no fun to be around."

Ambrose picked up the reins and gave me a sideways glance. "She spoils your fun?"

"I'd say so." I could feel my face scrunching into a frown. "She was positively rude to that handsome dark-haired one—Bob is his name. She told him Pa was a blacksmith who'd break him in half if he trifled with me."

Ambrose laughed again. "I'd say she gave Bob good advice."

I folded my arms across my chest. "There you go again, sticking up for Cordelia. Why? The two of you never got along. She was jealous because Pa liked you best."

He tilted his head, and his forehead wrinkled. "But you two used to be really close."

"Because I believed everything she said. Once Ma died and Aunt Hannah rushed us off to Westport to work in the hotel, I knew I couldn't trust her."

We were on the edge of town by then.

Ambrose cleared his throat. "Mrs. Collins asks about you girls all the time. I'm sure she'll want to hear all about your adventures."

He pulled the mules to a stop.

I sighed. "Not many adventures to tell. Just school and work and church. I did have fun at church activities, and Aunt May kept me up on the latest fashions, for all the good it did. Aunt Hannah called anything I liked too old for me."

He held out his hand, and I dismounted from the wagon. It was nice to have such a polite brother.

We entered the dining room from the street. On the far side of the room, I saw an open door that led to the hall where mostly men on the trail ate. We had pretty much the same setup at our hotel in Westport, a place for townspeople who wanted an evening out and a place for people who just needed a hot meal before they got back on the trail.

Pa was already seated at a table and frowning out the window. He turned his frown on us as we approached him.

"There you are," Pa said. "I wondered what was keeping you."

"Sorry," I said.

Even though daylight was fading, there were still people on the street. There was a "Closed" sign on the general store door, but the tavern was open. Mrs. Collins showed up, and we all stood to be polite. She hugged me before taking the chair next to mine.

A girl about Cordelia's age came for our order. Mrs. Collins suggested the meat loaf dinner, so I picked that. So did Ambrose. Pa took the fried chicken.

While we waited for our food, Pa asked about chores. "How did the milking go?"

"Slow. That's why we're late. I still remembered how, but my hands weren't used to the work. A dairy farmer brought milk to our hotel." I saw a chance to change the subject. "What about you, Mrs. Collins? Where do you get milk and butter for the boardinghouse?"

"My niece's husband, Mr. Clark, who also works for your father, has a farm now. He keeps me supplied with butter, milk, and eggs. A good arrangement for us both."

"I remember him and Mrs. Clark. They had a baby."

"Yes, he's four now. I'm sure you will be seeing the family at church."

The girl brought our meals and set them down, returning with a basket of yeast rolls and butter. I hesitated, not knowing whether there'd be a blessing, but Pa dug right in so I guessed he didn't pray in public. Lots of people didn't.

I took a bite of meat loaf. The spices were just right. "This is delicious," I said to Mrs. Collins. "Our cooks in Westport couldn't have done better."

"Thank you, dear. I understand your family's hotel has an excellent reputation. Occasionally, one of our guests will mention it."

I turned to Pa. "Hidden Springs has grown a lot. When Ambrose took me home, we went by the church and school. Ma would be really happy that Ella and Jennie will have a school to attend when they come home. How soon will that be?"

Pa carefully placed his knife on the edge of his plate and looked at me with narrowed eyes. "You asked that before, and I told you I can't say when that might be. You have to prove yourself, or those girls have to get big enough to pull their own weight. Whichever comes first, so this year or two years or three years."

I studied my plate. "They were awful sad they couldn't come. Ma would want us girls to be together."

"Well, someone has to take care of the place. Ambrose has the livery stable and part-time work at the shop, and you have the house. We'll see what happens."

So it was final. No way to wheedle anything out of him. I remembered now that he'd always been that way, but I had thought he might give just a little, knowing how badly my little sisters wanted to come home.

The talk for the rest of the meal was general, about the hotel, the farm, and Pa's shop and livery stable, plus a lot about Ambrose building the house and the things expected of me.

Pa placed a well-picked chicken bone on his plate and looked me full-on in the eyes. "You need to get on the house-decorating right away. I'll be inviting important men to discuss the wording of our state constitution. They need to be impressed."

On the ride home, I worried once again that I wouldn't be able to live up to Pa's expectations—the return of an old ache I had somehow forgotten during our years apart.

***

"Lucy, wake up." Ambrose's voice was hushed as he shook my shoulder.

I rolled onto my back and blinked.

Ambrose was using a lighted candle to ignite the wick of the lantern on my night table.

I glanced toward the window. It was still dark. "Why are you waking me at this hour?"

"Pa will be up in a few minutes and expect coffee and breakfast. You have to be up before him to get that ready."

I pushed back my blanket and rose up on my elbow. "Who did that before today?"

"I did." He shot me a satisfied smile. "But now we have you."

"And I thought you wanted me home because you missed my company."

"True, but I also thought it would be nice to have someone to take care of the house. One less job for me to do." He stood. "I'll leave you to get dressed."

He was halfway to the door when I called to him. "Ambrose."

He stopped. "What?"

"I'm worried. After last night, I'm not so sure I can live up to Pa's expectations."

"That's why I woke you, Luce. So you could get off on the right foot with Pa. See you in the kitchen. I'll show you how to work the stove."

I got out of bed and quickly straightened the covers before dressing. After giving my hair a few quick strokes with the brush, I hurried downstairs.

I hadn't been fast enough. Pa was already there.

Ambrose had started a fire in the stove and put the coffeepot on.

Pa scowled at me as I reached for the apron hanging on a wall peg. "You being here is supposed to free up Ambrose for other chores."

"Sorry, Pa," I said, taking the iron griddle Ambrose held out to me. I set it on the work table, lined the bottom with bacon, then carried it to the stove. "I overslept. I won't do that again."

He harrumphed and opened a newspaper. "Best not."

Before long the breakfast was cooked, devoured, and nothing was left but the dirty dishes and the list of chores for the day. It didn't matter that today was Sunday and there was church. The only one who rested on Sunday was Pa.

***

By the time we arrived at church, I was already worn out. I'd made the breakfast, washed the dishes, milked the cow, and carried the milk to the cellar for straining. I checked the milk from the night before and saw the cream was rising to the top. It still had time to go. Once I skimmed the cream from the top, I'd be hauling what milk we didn't use to the hogs. Just the thought made me tired.

Pa guided the team of horses to a place in the shade, and Ambrose helped me down from the wagon. He gave me his arm and escorted me into the church. I loved my big brother's manners. People greeted us in the vestibule. We stopped to sign our names. Then Ambrose escorted me to a pew two rows from the front where Mrs. Collins was seated there with her family.

The church impressed me. Four years ago, the mayor had conducted my mother's funeral service because the town did not have a minister. Now, besides the preacher, Hidden Springs had a new church and a choir. So much had happened in such a short time. It gave me something good to tell Ella and Jennie in tonight's letter.

After Reverend Sherwood preached the sermon, the ladies' group served a delicious meal on the lawn, and Pa introduced me to a town councilman who had moved to Hidden Springs while I was in Westport. The way the man looked at me, he was sizing me up to be his bride. I shivered at the thought. I found no fun in flirting when the end result might be an arranged marriage.

***

It was Sunday afternoon. With a break in my chores, I headed to the quiet of the cabin to write the promised letter to Ella and Jennie, wondering how I could make the events of the week sound positive.

> Dear Ella and Jennie,
>
> I miss you so much. Ambrose met me at the station and drove me home on one of our wagons from the livery stable. He showed me the house and brought in my trunk. Pa came later to make sure I had everything I needed in my room.
>
> About coming, dear sisters, that may be longer than I expected. It turns out the house is not entirely finished. Three of the bedrooms are complete with furnishings, and so is the kitchen, but the parlor, dining room, and library are without wall and floor

coverings and have no furniture besides Ma's rocker and buffet and a roll-top desk and chair. Pa wants me to pick out and order all furnishings for those rooms. Ambrose will do the work of putting everything together, but that will all take time, probably months. Pa says I have until the fall when he has invited some important men to the house.

So while you are waiting, I will send letters about our progress every week. As for you, work hard in school and mind Aunt Hannah.

Love,

Your sister, Lucy

Feeling like a liar, I folded, addressed, and sealed the letter. I had made it sound like they could come next summer when I knew it would be longer, probably when Pa found someone for me to marry.

I remembered how Aunt Hannah would often say she had escaped an arranged marriage because she was needed to take care of Grandma and the hotel. Maybe Pa wouldn't make me marry someone until Ella could take over the house for me. In his mind that would be four years from now. In the meantime, I had to keep house well enough to please him but not so well as to look like a good wife for any of his friends. And then, what about poor Ella? She would be next. Then Jennie. We girls were just grist for Pa's dynasty mill.

10) THE STAGE WEST

Cordelia

I was the first passenger to arrive at the Junction City stage station. I had hoped the men would not show up, but within a minute, grumbling male voices, including a curse word or two, filled the air.

"Dammit. It's too early for this nonsense," Bob Sims said.

"I have a headache," Scott Sims chimed in.

"Just shut up and get on the stage," Martin Sims ordered, but his cousins did neither, preferring to stand and complain.

I stared at the stage door. As first to arrive and having paid a premium fare, I had my pick of seats, but which would be best. I didn't want to risk a man on each side of me, so I decided to sit by one of the doors. I preferred to face west, the direction we would be going, so I could see the land coming up and have something to look at besides the men, but I'd heard that end had the bumpiest seat and that the dirt stirred up by the coach landed on the passengers sitting there. With that in mind, I selected the bench on the opposite end. It meant I would be looking at where I'd been, not something I liked to do, but the many travelers I had talked to at the hotel had assured me the seat closest to the driver's box was the best one to have.

I glanced up as my trunk, along with other baggage, was loaded on the top of the stage. The driver opened the door. I slid in first, turned sharply and took the seat I wanted, spread my skirts, and placed my handbag as a barrier between me and anyone who might sit next to me.

41

The two rowdies, Bob and Scott, boarded next. Bob gave me a sour look and took the bench nearest the back of the coach. Scott followed his lead. With plenty of room left for Martin, I hoped he would do the same. But my hopes were soon extinguished as he settled on the seat next to me.

"Good morning, Miss Pierce," he said.

I nodded curtly. "Mr. Sims."

Next, a man dressed in a black suit and vest with a white shirt, perhaps a preacher or a gambler, clambered in and took the seat on the opposite end of my bench, causing me to move my bag onto my lap and Martin's thighs to press against mine. No one wanted the middle bench.

But latecomers can't be choosers. A fancy woman in a low-cut, gold silk dress boarded next, took a look at the dwindling accommodations and took the middle seat facing the gambler. I supposed she spent enough time with such men that he appeared to be a kindred spirit. Finally, a woman with a baby on her hip nudged a girl of about five ahead of her. Seeing the crowd, she sighed, put the girl next to the saloon woman, and piled two bags between her feet on the floor.

The driver called to someone, "Full coach. You'll have to sit on top."

I sat scrunched against the side and wondered if he would let me do the same. The only good thing about the current arrangement was that I couldn't see Bob and Scott because of the people between us. And then, wouldn't you know, Scott got chivalrous.

"Ma'am." Scott tapped the mother on the shoulder. "You're going to get bounced right off that seat. My brother and I will trade with you."

"We will?" Bob sounded shocked at the declaration.

Scott's nod was decisive. "Indeed, we will."

At last, everyone and everything was loaded, making me wonder how the mules could possibly pull such a load, but soon the driver cracked the whip, and we swayed, lurched, and braced to keep to our seats.

Scott's knees hit mine and Martin fell against me.

I shuddered. It was going to be a long trip to Denver.

***

With Martin pressed against my right side and Scott's knees

knocking mine, I had more male contact than I had previously encountered. The miles swayed by, the coach dipping and bouncing. The little girl giggled during such times, clearly enjoying the ride. I could barely see her through the occasional space between Bob and Scott. The fancy woman looked to be in her thirties although it was hard to tell with the rouge on her face. She held tightly to her strap, but Bob often rocked against her. She laughed him off as though he were an annoying child, flirted, rolled her eyes at the gambler across from her as if to say "What can I do?"

I couldn't see the gambler's face, but his voice was deep and smooth. "What is your destination, Miss . . .?"

"Where else? Denver City," the fancy woman said. "I hear it's booming with miners and their gold, and very few women to talk with at the end of a hard stint of prospecting. And you?"

"The same. Wherever there are miners, there are men wanting to bet. It's the best way to get gold without getting my hands dirty."

The mother in the back seat sniffed her disapproval. I reckoned she was glad Scott had offered to exchange seats. Bob, who had at first protested, seemed downright pleased with his ability to jostle the fancy woman.

The gambler raised his voice. "Anyone getting off before we reach Denver City?"

"I am," said the woman with children. "My husband has a home station we should reach this evening."

I peered between Bob and Scott in an attempt to see her. "A home station? What is that?"

"One where the stage stops overnight. You can get a meal at a home station. The swing stations are in between. No meals. A few minutes to change teams and stretch. Then off to the next stop."

The gambler leaned forward so he could see me. "Are you new to stage travel, Miss . . . ?"

I reckoned he was collecting everyone's names since we would be traveling together for eight to ten days, so I answered. "Miss Pierce. And you are?"

"Grant Parsons, at your service." He touched the brim of his black hat and nodded.

I bit my lip, suppressing a smile, remembering I had figured him for a gambler or a parson, and here he was, a combination: a gambler named Parsons. "Mr. Parsons." I nodded in a formal greeting.

"You look young to be traveling alone, Miss Pierce. Are you going to meet your parents?"

Scott interrupted. "Her pa's in Hidden Springs, back before Junction City. To hear her tell it, he's a blacksmith who will break any feller in two who messes with his daughter."

Bob put in his opinion. "Miss Pierce don't need no pa to protect her. She's got more spikes than a porky pine."

Martin Sims jumped in at that point. "No need to be rude because Miss Pierce isn't interested in your attentions."

Bob laughed. "Nobody put any attentions toward her. It was that pretty sister we wanted to get to know."

The fancy woman offered her opinion. "Don't pay no mind to these yahoos. With the woman shortage in mining towns, you'll be married in no time. Be sure to find someone who's got money and knows how to hold on to it. Keep him away from the likes of this fella here." She pointed a finger at Mr. Parsons.

I smiled. "That sounds like excellent advice, Miss—I didn't catch your name."

"I didn't throw it. But I suppose if we're all going to be bouncing down the road in close quarters, a name is the least familiar thing we'll be sharing. Sadie Jones."

I nodded. "Miss Jones."

"Sadie will do." She turned her attention to the gambler. "Mr. Parsons, seems I've heard of you. St. Louis and the riverboats maybe? Or was it San Francisco?"

"I've had the pleasure of visiting both cities."

"You have a reputation for winning."

"One cannot be a professional for long if one does not win."

We went over another bump, sending us all at least two inches off our seats. The baby, possibly a year old, seated at his mother's side, knocked his head against the back of the seat and let out an angry wail.

All conversation stopped while she tended him. I realized we knew her destination, but not her name.

***

The first station we came to consisted of two tents twenty-some miles out of Junction City. While the driver changed out the mules, we passengers stepped out of the stage to stretch our limbs. I looked around at the mules being picketed on grass and the rail pen holding two cows. The grass was thinner here and the white limestone had given way to sandstone. I looked out across a prairie that seemed endless.

We spent the night at the next station, sleeping in the coach. The station itself had two tents and a log house half built. This is where the mother and two children got off, giving the rest of us more room to stretch out. Bob and Scott reclaimed the seat they had relinquished to the mother and children, and Sadie stretched out on the middle bench, which left the gambler, Martin Sims, and me scrunched together on the back seat. The problem with the middle seat was there was a bit of a back but no sides to lean against. The seat was narrow with no room for two people to lie down, which was what Sadie had done.

Through lidded eyes, I watched the men watch her, looking for a switch in her position that would allow them a glimpse of more bosom or limb.

When we were ready to leave the next morning, the second coach joined us. Not weighted down with freight or other passengers, it could travel faster and be on the lookout for Indians or robbers, while also waiting for us at the next station. If we didn't show up in a reasonable time, it could come looking for us.

That gave me a sense of security, but I couldn't help wishing I could ride in that coach even though I saw the wisdom of the company not allowing it.

Our midday meal, chicken and noodles in a thin broth, was served at the next station. We placed tin plates on the top of a freighting box and sat on nail kegs.

We were a couple of miles out of the station when the men spotted a group of three wagons headed east. One had a word in black on the side. Bob, Scott, and Martin were stretching their necks to get a good look.

"Busted," Bob read. "What's that about?"

Mr. Parsons nodded at the bedraggled wagons passing by. "Those are go-backers, men who came without the money and the knowhow for prospecting. The guidebooks told them gold could be scooped up by the shovelful. However, that is rarely the case. Mining is hard work, and it takes more than a gold pan and a pick and shovel to get at the richest ore."

"Well, that won't happen to us," Bob said. "Our pa's laid claim to a rich vein, so we got a head start on those just rushing out here on an idea."

"We're not supposed to talk about that." Scott gritted his teeth. "How many times do I have to tell you?"

Bob frowned and drew himself up, folding his arms across his chest. "What? You think any of these three can take our mine."

Martin chimed in. "They might know someone who could. Your father doesn't need a bunch of latecomers flooding in filling the land up with miners staking claims."

Scott watched until the three wagons had passed. "They looked pretty broken. I wonder what happened?"

"Whatever it was," Sadie said, "at least they'll probably make it home from here. They are almost back to civilization."

Throughout the day, we continued to come upon go-backers, an almost steady stream at times, the men as worn and tattered as their animals and wagons.

That night, we stopped by a creek to camp. Seeing a grave marker, I crossed the campground and stood beside it to read the words painted on a rock: Sam Field, born and died, April, 1859.

The sight of that tiny grave hit me. I swallowed hard, and my throat closed. All I could think of was Ma and her dead babies. I squeezed my eyes shut, trying to push the memory away and keep tears from falling.

I felt a hand on my arm.

"Are you all right, Miss Pierce?"

Martin Sims seemed to be paying me a lot of attention, annoyingly so.

"I'm fine," I said. "Seeing this tiny grave makes me think of how many young lives are lost because men take foolish chances with their lives. Then they blame the women for the loss of the children with questions like 'what did she do wrong?' and 'why isn't she strong enough?' You all want to go on adventures and don't stop to think about your families at all."

"You seem to have some experience with that."

"I wish never to see another baby dead because of a reckless father, and yet I know I will." I spun around and hurried away, seeking a place by the shallow creek to sit and listen and watch the slow-moving water.

***

46

We left the camp at daybreak as usual and had passed the first station and change of mules, when Bob yelled, "Buffalo," like we were all hard of hearing.

Scott leaned across Bob to look out the window. "Where?"

Sadie Jones, in her middle seat, held on to the strap and leaned forward as the coach swayed over the uneven ground. We were climbing a slow rise. When we reached the top, her eyes widened. "Oh, my! It's like an ocean of brown waves."

I sat crunched in my corner, unable to see the animals from my seat.

The second coach had been ahead. It came back, and both drivers stopped. Our driver called down. "You folks can get out and stretch if you want."

We did.

Sadie and Grant were the first off, then Bob and Scott. Martin followed them and turned to assist me as I gathered my skirts. I longed for the freedom I'd had when dressed as a boy or even the freedom bloomers gave. But going into a new area and not knowing the conflict my clothing might cause, I decided being traditional was best. But I did have bloomers as well as my boy clothes in my satchel.

As I rounded the coach to the north side, I saw what had the other passengers standing open-mouthed and wide-eyed, focused on the distance. Sadie had been right. It was like seeing an ocean of brown waves.

"Lucky they're past the road," the driver said. "I hope the folks at the home station are okay."

"Why wouldn't they be?" Martin asked.

The driver shook his head. "Herd like that stampedes, it runs over anything in its path, station, coach, anything. People get trampled."

I shivered. I had worried about robbers and Indians but hadn't given a thought to being run down by buffalo, which seemed a far worse fate than being robbed or kidnapped.

We heard gunshots in the distance and the waving backs of the sea of animals picked up.

"Hunters," Grant Parsons said. "Kill the buffalo and leave their bodies to rot." He spit on the ground.

***

We stopped at the Prairie Dog Creek station for the night. The wind whipped at my dress, the pieces of lead sewn in the hem to keep my skirts from flying up pounded my legs. We still had five days to go before reaching Denver, and tempers were growing short, at least mine was.

Boredom had set in among the men. Tired of bedeviling me, they turned to gambling. They bet on anything from what animal they would see next to how long before we spotted the next traveler to Zion or the next go-backer. Within a day, they shifted to cards and increasingly higher bets.

Scott won the first two hands of poker, then an occasional hand, enough to keep him in the game. Martin was the most reserved and Bob the most volatile, cursing every time he lost, which was most of the time.

By evening, they had switched from cards to dice, spreading a blanket on the ground in front of the fire, shouting excitedly over numbers I was unfamiliar with.

Sadie Jones, the fancy woman, looked on, sighed, and shook her head. "Fools don't know when to quit."

I had avoided any lengthy talks with Sadie, seeing the business she was in, but I was so bored, conversation with her began to look good.

I took a seat on a nail keg next to hers. "Five more days," I said. "Do you think we'll make it without someone getting shot?"

Sadie chuckled. "Hard to tell." She brushed her hand across her silk skirt. "What made you decide to come down off that high horse?"

"Couldn't bear talking to myself any longer, so I listened around for another voice." I nodded at the ring of dice throwers. "None of theirs sounded good."

"I don't know. That Martin would like to talk."

"To me?" That was hard to believe. Martin was the least annoying of the group—well, except for the gambler—but neither man seemed interested in me.

"Every time Bob aims a smart aleck remark your way, Martin tries to shut him up." She put her foot on a rock and leaned her elbow on her knee. "That says something."

"That he has better manners than his cousins, which isn't saying much."

"Well, they're young. Bob, now, I'd say is seventeen, maybe

eighteen. About your age." She raised an eyebrow.

"Seventeen," I said.

"Seventeen." She stared off into the endless prairie. "That sick friend must be important for you to travel through all this wasteland. He'll likely be dead or well by the time you reach Denver City."

"Her name's Miz Wilma," I said, correcting her assumption that my friend was male. "She helped me when I ran away four years ago. I ruined my shoes and cut up my feet walking barefoot on the prairie, and she came along with her wagon full of herbs and doctored my feet and gave me a ride. I might not have made it without her."

In the distance, I heard the rumbling grunt of buffalo. "You reckon they're coming this way?" I asked.

"Don't know. This is my first experience seeing herds as big as the ones we've seen the past couple of days."

"But you talked about being in San Francisco. How'd you get all the way across the country and not see them?"

She laughed. "There's more than one way to get to California, and one of them is a whole lot easier than crossing hundreds of miles of prairie and mountains."

"What's that?"

"By boat, of course. I was about your age when I took a ship out of New Orleans, went down to Panama and crossed the land on foot and by boat to the Pacific Ocean and took another ship to San Francisco."

"Now you say it, I remember hearing of folks doing that, but I'd forgotten. I've spent my whole life watching wagons go west. It seemed like that was the way everybody got there."

"Back to you. You said something about your father breaking some bones if those boys got too smart with you. How does he feel about you traveling alone?"

I thought about lying, but then I figured we were never going to see each other after this trip was over, so I might as well say it outright. Besides, if I found my real father, I'd be explaining something about it to him, so I might as well get some practice.

"It wasn't my pa I was talking about. It was Lucy's. She's my half-sister. Before my ma married Hiram, she fell for a man who promised her marriage. Then he took off, but not before he left her with me. So she had to marry Hiram to save the family's reputation. Hiram never let me forget that."

My voice turned gravelly, and I clasped my hands, remembering the day Hiram had caught me splashing water on my camisole, trying to cool off, and the way he'd looked at me, his eyes lighting up and lips stretching into a lecherous smile.

"You said you ran away from home when you were thirteen. Your stepfather have anything to do with that?"

"How'd you guess?"

"I know men. It's my job." She brushed her skirt with her hand. "So are you really going to Denver City to take care of a sick friend, or are you going to look for this missing father?"

I stared at her. "How did you know?"

"I know young girls without fathers. Lots of them. I've even been one. Trying to find what's missing is what we do."

***

We were stretching our legs at a swing station. It was windy, hot, no trees, and sandy soil with little grass. There were no animals in this dry land, save a gopher now and then.

Grant Parsons squinted into the distance. "There's the Rockies," he said.

I followed his gaze and saw nothing but a huge cloud bank that stretched the entire length of the western horizon. "Where?"

"Right in front of you, Miss Pierce. Don't let the clouds fool you. The mountains are there, too. The tallest ones you've likely ever seen."

"The only ones I've ever seen." I squinted, straining my eyes for the sight that would signal that the end of the wearisome journey was at hand. "But I don't see them."

"You will."

By the time we stopped for the night, I did. The bottoms were dark and wide. At the top, snow and clouds mingled. Their size amazed me.

***

Sleeping sitting up, jammed against the side of the coach, had my shoulders stiff and sore. I glanced at Sadie, stretched out on the middle bench and once more deplored my choice of seat. I wiggled my shoulders, my movements enough to jostle Martin's head and cause it to fall back. He began emitting loud snores, his limbs spreading and pressing against me. If I hadn't been convinced he was sleeping, I would have slapped him for being fresh.

Ever since Sadie had mentioned Martin was interested in me, I had been paying more attention. I thought she might be right, but I was not interested in him. Under normal circumstances, I probably never would have given him more than a passing "hello." I subscribed to Aunt Hannah's idea of not becoming involved with a man unless he felt the same about a woman's rights as I did. Martin seemed too traditional for my suffragette opinions. I smiled at the thought of what his reaction would be if I changed into the bloomer trousers and matching knee-length dress packed in my trunk.

I sighed at the thought of putting on clean clothes. I was wearing the same dress I'd put on over a week ago when I left Junction City, the last place I'd slept in a bed. I imagined that I smelled as bad as I had when Miz Wilma had picked me up on that hillside four years ago.

I wondered how she was doing with her broken leg. I hoped it was healing, but also hoped she hadn't left Denver City. Without her direction, I didn't know how I might find my father, Justin Quinn. Panning for gold wasn't much to go on since there were thousands of men doing that.

I remembered telling Aunt Hannah I was being stupid to search for him, but she'd told me I wasn't, that I had a right to find out for myself how my father felt about me.

I squirmed again. One more night in this crowded coach. And then what? The stage ticket had taken most of my savings of the last four years. I had maybe two weeks to search for my father before I ran out of money. Of course, Aunt Hannah would send my fare home if need be, but that would take weeks, and I didn't want to ask. I was seventeen, old enough to take care of myself. And I had skills. I had run the hotel by myself a few days when Aunt Hannah toured with the suffragettes, speaking to groups, trying to get a woman's right to vote written into the Kansas constitution. I could find work if I had to.

11) SETTLING IN

Lucy

Within three days, I had settled into a bone-wearying, mind-numbing routine of getting up before dawn, cooking the meals, milking the cow, and feeding the livestock, including the chickens, the cow, and the pigs, cleaning the house, and working in the garden. Today, I was doing laundry for the first time. When building the house, Ambrose had included a lean-to that sheltered the wash tubs from the sun while allowing a breeze to blow through, moving the heat from the fire away, making the process a bit more bearable. Today, I had cut the number of petticoats I wore from six to three because of the heat. Now, as I worked the plunger up and down and thought of wringing water from the yards of material in those undergarments, I decided to forget fashion altogether when I was doing chores.

By the end of the first day home, I realized I had highly over-estimated my housekeeping abilities. While I had lived in a hotel for four years and worked a number of jobs, I'd never had to do everything at once—alone. Others were always about to lend a hand. I had never cooked an entire meal by myself in all that time. I peeled potatoes and other vegetables for soups and stews, kneaded bread, rolled pie crusts, and frosted cakes. But others were present to put the vegetables into huge pots and add meat and spices, to put the bread and pies in ovens and remove them when done, to mix and bake the cakes. Where I might dust and sweep rooms or change beds, someone else mopped the floors and washed the sheets. And above all, there was someone to talk to, to make a joke that lightened the load of the chores. Here on the farm, there was no one. I ached for the sound of a female voice.

As if on cue, a female voice called out, "Hello! Anyone home?"

"Here." I tossed aside the wooden plunger I had been using to wash trousers and shirts, wiped my hands, and raced around the side of the house toward the front.

A pretty girl about my age with blond hair, brown eyes, and a big smile met me half way. She held out a tin plate containing a pie.

"I thought it was time to come welcome my new neighbor," she said. "Is this a bad time?"

"I'm doing the wash, but I can let the clothes soak a while. Let's go inside."

"My name's Susan. I heard you're Lucy."

"Yes. So we're neighbors. Where do you live?"

"The first cabin down the road toward town. I'm not sure your pa likes us being so close."

I rolled my eyes. "He wants to own everything he can see from here, I reckon, and when I look out an upstairs window, I can see your place." I opened the back door and led the way into the kitchen, glad I'd cleared up all the dishes and everything was in good order. I motioned toward the table. "Have a seat. Would you like some water? That's all I have—unless you'd like milk." I eyed the pie tin and thought about how good pie topped with cream would taste. Then I thought about Pa and Ambrose, but they weren't here. I'd have my piece now, and they could have the rest later.

I took two plates from the cupboard, set them on the counter, and reached in the drawer for a knife. Before I could cut through the crust, the door knocker sounded.

I put the knife aside. My! No guests for three days and then two in one afternoon. "I'll be right back."

When I opened the door, I looked into the most gorgeous brown eyes ever. The boy whose face they were in had a smile that matched his eyes. "Hi, I'm looking for my sister Susan. She said something about coming here."

"She's here," I said, wondering why he hadn't just come with her if he wanted to visit.

He held up a pail. "She was supposed to pick strawberries for shortcake tonight, but she forgot this."

I stepped back. "Come in. She's in the kitchen." I eyed the pail. "You folks cook a lot of desserts. I was about to cut into the pie Susan brought when you knocked."

"Susan's one of the best cooks around. The church is having a pie-baking contest and sale this weekend to raise money for new hymn books. You going to enter a pie?"

"I'll have to think on it. Susan's entry will be hard to beat."

Susan looked up as we entered the kitchen and raised her eyebrows when she saw her brother. "Willy, are you following me?"

"No. I already knew where you were going. You forgot the bucket for the strawberries."

"Willy, is it?" I asked. "You forgot to tell me your name." I crossed to the counter and cut the pie in half and then one half into thirds and brought the servings to the table.

"Yes, Miss Pierce. Willy's my name."

"You may call me Lucy."

He settled on a chair across from Susan. "So, Lucy, how do you like Hidden Springs after a big place like Westport?"

"This town's grown so much it actually looks big to me. We were one of the first families to settle here." I laughed. "I bet you've heard that before because my pa's pretty proud of it."

Susan smiled. "We have."

"I got a quick look around when Ambrose met me at the stage. Also, we came back to eat at the boardinghouse that evening. Except for that, I've been catching up on the work needing done around here."

We talked for a few minutes about them coming to Hidden Springs, their pa's farming, and their ma's needlework.

The clock struck one. I had been visiting for thirty minutes and the laundry was still soaking. "I'm sorry to run you all off, but I have to finish the wash or it won't get dry before Pa gets home. Perhaps I'll see you all at church."

"We'll be looking for you," Willy said.

I removed the plates from the table, and we all walked out the back door. I waved to them as they crossed the field toward the creek that divided our property. When I picked up the plunger, I found the water had cooled, so it was a good thing this was my last load of the day.

***

54

Pa appreciated the pie Susan brought us but not the fact that I shared it with her and her brother.

"Someone brings a gift, they shouldn't eat half of it," he said and shoveled in another forkful.

I folded my hands in my lap and stared at them. "I had a piece too, Pa. That's why the rest is for you and Ambrose."

He propped his elbow on the table and shook his fork at me. "And that boy. Willy. You shouldn't have let him in the house with me and your brother not at home. He'll be thinking he can come back any time he wants. Give you a bad reputation letting the likes of him in the door."

I kept my eyes on my hands. "His sister was here."

"I have to wonder why. Oh, yeah. I've seen her looking at Ambrose. Probably thinking she can marry up in the world. Well, neither of those Hogan brats is good enough for either of you."

I looked at Ambrose, expecting him to say something, but his eyes studied his plate while he scooped pie into his mouth.

I clasped my fingers and stroked one thumb with the other. "Susan told me the church was having a fundraiser, a pie-baking contest. Are we going to that?" I asked, hoping to change the subject. After all, Pa was interested in anything having to do with civic duties.

Pa nodded. "I reckon we will. What kind of pie you baking?"

That question made me sorry I'd mentioned the contest. "I'm not real used to the oven yet. I'm not sure how good a pie I could bake."

He dropped his fork on the plate and stared at me, shaking his head. "What? You worked in a hotel for four years and can't bake a pie? What did Hannah have you doing?"

"The ovens in the hotel are a lot bigger. I need to get used to ours."

"You got that right. The biscuits you made this morning were too brown on top and not done in the middle. You'd best get to practicing. Man wants a woman knows how to cook." He took a last forkful of pie, chewed, and swallowed. "We got some jars of canned peaches. Practice your pie-making on those. The Hogan girl specializes in apple. So do most of the other women. You need something different."

"Yes, Pa."

"And like I said, don't be having company when I'm not home. You got your chores to tend to."

I imagined what I would have said if Aunt Hannah had talked to me the way he just did. I would have told her off. I would have said I had a right to friends. But, really, I couldn't imagine Aunt Hannah speaking to me like that.

I stifled a sob. Nothing was going like I thought it would. Pa was right about the biscuits. I wasn't as good at housekeeping and cooking as I'd thought.

I got up from the table and cleared the dishes. Then I went out to do the milking and was furiously tugging at the cow's teats when Ambrose squatted beside me.

"You okay?" he asked.

I sniffled and glanced at him. "What makes you think I'm not?"

"You seemed ready to bust in there with Pa going on about not letting people in the house."

I stopped milking for a second and used my arm to wipe sweat from my forehead. "I hadn't seen anyone but you and Pa for three days. I was so happy Susan came calling. I thought I'd have a friend, but now Pa doesn't want her here. What's he got against her?"

"He thinks we like each other, and he doesn't think she's good enough for me—just like he doesn't think Willy is good enough for you."

That's what Pa had said. I shook my head. "But it's years before we marry anybody."

Ambrose picked up a piece of straw and fiddled with it. "Me, maybe. I reckon you'll be tying the knot sooner."

That stopped me cold. I stared at him. "How much sooner?"

"Maybe a year or so from now."

"I'm going to have to talk to Pa. No one's shown any interest in courting me." The thought of Bob Sims and his flirting made me smile. Still, flirting wasn't the same as having a suitor.

Ambrose broke the straw in half and tossed it aside. "Don't you know by now Pa's not someone you talk to; he's someone you listen to."

I took up furious milking again, the liquid hitting the edge of the pail, my chest heaving as I understood the true reason for Pa wanting me home. He wanted to marry me off to one of his wealthy, influential friends. Probably, he'd never intended for Ella and Jennie to come to live here—at least not until they were old enough to marry off, too. And it was almost time for me to write to them again.

I had promised a letter a week, like Ambrose had written to me. What was I going to say? They had such high hopes because of all the things I had imagined and told them as truth before I had come home and found out different.

***

I stood at the side of the pigpen with yet another peach pie disaster in hand, thankful that I had two pigs to destroy all signs of my failed baking. I raised the pie tin to dump the contents and stopped myself. Although I wanted to get rid of my failure, I needed it to find out what I was doing wrong and what I had to do to make a better pie.

It was already Friday. I had only one more day to produce two edible pies: one for the contest judging and the other for the sale. No matter what I did, I couldn't seem to get any part of the pie right, not the thickening or the spices or the crust. How did Susan do it? Wondering if she'd share her tips with me, I took off my apron, put a jar of peaches and the pie in a basket, and headed toward her house, hoping she'd be home. Pa had said she couldn't visit me. He hadn't said I couldn't visit her.

When I arrived at Susan's cabin, the door was wide open. I called out a "hello."

Susan came to greet me, her hair pulled back in a long braid and flour on her hands. "Lucy. Hi. What's that in the basket?"

"Not a treat," I said. "It's my awful peach pie. Soggy. I know I shouldn't ask advice when you're entering the contest. You'll probably win from all I hear, but I don't want to enter a pie that embarrasses my pa and has him telling me no man will ever marry someone who is as bad a cook as I am."

Susan laughed. "Well, I wouldn't want that to happen. Come on in, and we'll take a look at the pie. What kind is it?"

"Peach."

She stepped back so I could enter. I saw a woman in a rocker with her lap full of yellow crochet yarn. She looked up and smiled.

Susan gestured toward her. "This is my mother. Ma, this is Lucy Pierce from down the road."

"Nice to meet you, Mrs. Hogan," I said.

"Likewise, Lucy. Excuse me for not getting up, but as you can see, my lap is full at the moment. Making a blanket for my first grandchild who'll be arriving next month."

"The first. You must be excited." I held up my basket. "I came hoping Susan could help me bake a decent pie."

"She's the expert all right. Ever since she started baking three years ago, I leave it all to her."

The inside of their home reminded me of our old cabin, except they had a fine cast iron cook stove in the kitchen area.

"I was fixing to make my apple pies for tomorrow. Let me get them ready for the oven, and we'll have a look at yours."

She dumped the apple filling, smelling of nutmeg and cinnamon, into the pie shells, then folded an already rolled out top crust and placed it over one of the pies. She pressed the edges together, cut a half moon slit in the center and then additional tiny jabs on either side. After sprinkling a mixture of sugar and cinnamon on top, she moved on to repeat the process for the second pie.

Her pies assembled, she handed me a folded towel. "Open the oven for me."

I did. She slid the pies onto the rack, and I closed the door.

"Now, let's see what you brought," she said.

I removed the towel cover from the basket and brought out the jar of peaches and the failed pie. "I thought it would help if you saw the fruit I was using as well as the finished product."

Her eyes narrowed as she inspected the pie. "I see you cut it."

I gazed down at the mess in the pan. I had removed a piece earlier, which is when I saw that the filling had not set up. Juice had run all over the bottom of the pan. "That's how I knew how bad it was."

"How long did you let it cool before cutting?"

"Half an hour or so."

"Not long enough. One to two hours is best. You have to give time for the filling to cool and set up." She picked up the jar of peaches. "These look good."

"Pa bought them somewhere. Ma used to make really good peach pies. She jotted down notes about how much of each ingredient, but not the whole recipe, so I'm guessing about what to do."

"Did you drain the juice off before mixing in the spices and thickener?"

"No."

She picked up a spoon and scooped up a bite of peach and juice and tasted it. Nodding, she said, "Tastes good."

She broke off a piece of the crust from around the top of the pan and put it in her mouth.

I winced, knowing it wasn't good. "Tough, huh?"

"A little. Try mixing a teaspoon of vinegar in the dough before you roll it out." She smiled. "So you need to drain the peaches before mixing in the spices, add vinegar to the dough before rolling it out, and let the pie cool at least two hours before cutting."

"Do you think that will be enough for a passable pie?"

She squinted and nodded. "Should be."

I put the pie and peaches in the basket. "Thanks so much, Susan. I'd better get back home and start baking for tomorrow. It was nice to meet you, Mrs. Hogan."

"Come any time, Lucy. We enjoy company."

As I was walking out the door, I ran into Willy.

His mouth stretched into a wide smile. "Hello, Miss Pierce. What brings you here?"

"The need for your sister's pie-baking advice," I said. "Pa insists I take part in the contest and bake sale tomorrow."

Willy's eyebrows shot up. "I'll be sure to bid on your pie."

My face felt hot. "Best see how it turns out first." I hurried off toward my house.

***

I made a single pie first, so I could see if all Susan's hints had helped. I inhaled the sweet smell of cinnamon, nutmeg, and cloves as I took the pie out of the oven and set it on the iron trivet to cool. It would be two hours before I could cut in and find out if it was fit to show anyone. Pa and Ambrose would be home by then, wanting their supper. I'd have to bake the pies for the sale tonight.

What if this one didn't turn out any better than the others? Well, Willy said he'd buy one, so I wouldn't be completely embarrassed. At least, not until he took a bite. But what would Pa do if Willy bought my pie? I should have told Willy not to bid.

I stood staring at the pie for at least five minutes before I told myself staring wouldn't do any good. Time would pass faster if I worked on supper.

I checked on the chicken I'd been stewing and then went to the garden for greens. I'd fix noodles and add fresh peas and carrots. When I got to the garden, I saw weeds had sprung up among the carrots. I sank to the ground and pulled the intruders, my breath heaving. How could weeds have come up so fast? I had spent the last couple of days trying to bake a decent pie. There wasn't enough time to do everything expected of me. I yanked a dandelion and threw it to the edge of the garden. Getting up, I stumbled from the rows of vegetables, not even watching my step, until I reached the edge and turned around, my eyes focusing on a trail of smashed plants. The sight brought back that day the slave hunters had come through, wrecking our house and riding horses through the garden. Ma had gathered Ella and Jennie and me into her arms and held us as we shook in fear, wondering if they would beat us or kill us. Wondering if all the bad stuff would make Ma lose the baby. But then they rode away, leaving wreckage behind them, and we sat there, not knowing what to do. Then Ma let out a happy "Oh" and touched her stomach. "Feel," she'd said. "Feel your brother kick."

We sat there, holding each other and feeling the life inside Ma until she finally said, "Well, we may as well go see how bad it is."

And we did. And it was bad. And before we could clean anything up, Ambrose ran in and told us Pa was hurt. That's when everything got too much. I hadn't been able to keep up with the work then, and Ma died. And I couldn't do everything now. Nobody was going to die because of it, but Pa was going to be mad. He wasn't going to bring Ella and Jennie home like I had promised them. I had told them I could do everything, and I couldn't even bake a decent pie. I hugged my knees to my chest, rested my forehead on them, my mind whirling with images of my failures and what Pa would say about them until, finally, my eyes closed, and I gave in to tears and exhaustion.

***

"Lucy. Hey, Lucy. What are you doing out here?"

I blinked and looked up. My cheeks felt stiff from dried tears. "Oh, my, I fell asleep. What time is it? Is Pa home?"

"It's time for supper, and Pa's wants to know where it is. He's washing up now."

I glanced around the garden. I'd picked enough greens for salad, but there was no time now for peas or carrots to cook. We could eat the carrots raw, but Pa would complain. He didn't care for rabbit food.

I got to my feet, picked up the basket of vegetables, and rushed to the house. I checked the chicken. Thankfully, it hadn't boiled dry.

I took the cooked bird from the pot and removed the bones. Then I thickened the broth to make gravy. I had made extra biscuits that morning, so I spooned gravy over them and the chicken.

Pa came in from washing up and glared at the meal. "What's this mess?"

"I'm sorry," I said. "I got so busy making the pie I forgot about fixing side dishes."

"This it?" He squinted at the pie and bent to take a whiff. "Smells good. Where's the other one?"

"I made this one for you to try first. See if anything needs improved. I'll make the ones for church after supper." I decided not to mention the six pies the pigs had fed on.

He pulled out his chair and sat. "Well, then. Get supper on the table. The quicker we eat, the sooner we can get to the pie."

I breathed a sigh of relief. "Supper coming up."

After the meal was over, I brought the pie to the table and cut it in half and then that half into thirds.

"If that's as good as it looks," Pa said, "I may have to have seconds."

Stunned at the compliment, I fought to keep from gaping as I slipped the pie server under a slice and slid the pastry onto his plate. He immediately pressed a fork through it and took a bite while I fixed a piece for Ambrose.

Pa nodded his head in satisfaction. "Now, that is good pie. You use your ma's recipe?"

"I did."

"Thought so. She made a good pie. That Susan down the road has some strong competition."

I swallowed hard. I hoped he wouldn't badmouth Susan's pie-making skills at church since she was the one who helped me figure out what I was doing wrong.

12) DENVER CITY

Cordelia

The stage rumbled into Denver. My twelve-day trip from Westport was at last at an end. I wanted a bath and a change of clothes more than I ever had, but I was reluctant to spend the money for a hotel room and anxious to find Miz Wilma.

As the driver helped me step down from the coach, I said, "I need to make arrangements to leave my trunk here until I secure lodging. Can the station clerk help me with that?"

"Yes, ma'am. I'll set your trunk inside the storeroom."

"Thank you."

I entered the station, a red brick building, and joined the line. By the time it was my turn, I had spotted a hotel sign across the street, a two-story wood frame building. I was dirty and tired and wanted to clean up. I decided to get a room if one was available before looking for Miz Wilma.

When it was my turn, I asked the stationmaster for directions. "I'm looking for a friend, Miz Wilma. She's staying with the Russell family. Can you give me directions to their place or tell me who I might ask?"

"Miz Wilma? The old healer with the broken leg? She's set up about half a mile down and then about the same distance west toward the mountains."

"Thank you." After making arrangements for the storage of my trunk, I carried my satchel containing two changes of clothes and toiletries across the street to the hotel. The desk clerk said they had a room on the second floor.

I signed the ledger and received a key and directions to the room, along with matches to light the lantern. After requesting a pitcher of water be delivered, I headed for the stairs. On my way, I paused in front of a sign that read "Dining Hall" and peered in. The room looked and sounded more like a saloon, with the all-male clientele crowded around tables of various sizes, playing cards and shooting dice. Only a half dozen tables along the wall were occupied by men eating. There was shouting throughout as someone won or lost. Two men jostled me before pausing to look me up and down, their eyes reminding me of Hiram's leering shine the day he found me cooling off in the creek. My stomach growled with hunger, but getting a meal here was impossible. I went on to my room, worried about what accommodations I might find there. Outside the door to my room, a lantern sat on a shelf. I used one of the matches to light it and unlocked the door.

My worries were justified. The stench of tobacco, whiskey, and sweat emanating from the cramped cubicle assaulted my nose. Stale smoke hung in the air, stinging my eyes. Seeing what appeared to be a window on the outside wall, I crossed to it, pushed the wooden slat open, and propped it up with a board. Pressing my face close to the opening, I filled my lungs with fresh air. Hoping the room would air out, I stepped away from the window and took in the furnishings. A bed of sorts made of board slats on top of nail kegs stood along one wall. After inspecting the mattress, I concluded it was straw stuffed into a stained cotton ticking. The two woolen blankets smelled of tobacco and sweat but seemed free of vermin.

My impulse was to leave, but where would I go? This was a new mining town. Other accommodations, if there were any, might be worse. I did not know Miz Wilma's situation, and I did not want to inconvenience those who were caring for her. Best to stay here. It was only for one night.

There was a knock at the door. A voice called out, "Are you there, ma'am? I've brought your water."

I let the boy in. He placed a large pitcher of warm water on the dresser beside a basin. I gave him a nickel tip, and as soon as he left, I slid the bolt on the door, locking it.

A basin bath was not what I had been longing for, but it would have to do. I cleaned up quickly, wishing I could wash my hair, but there was no way to do that with so little water.

While choosing what to wear, I looked longingly at my bloomers, but passed on them. I would save them for the mountains. No sense stirring up animosity before I had to.

Refreshed, I set out on foot, noticing that the sun had touched the mountaintops to the west. Daylight was fading fast. In the flatlands, the evening light seemed to go on for hours. Here, once the sun slipped below the mountains, daylight was all but gone. I passed what looked like an eating house, but given the coming dark, I hurried past it, my stomach growling. Before long, I came to Miz Wilma's wagon set up beside a tent and a half-built cabin. I hoped someone would be around to accompany me to the hotel since walking alone at night seemed risky. My only comfort was the derringer I carried in my handbag.

I approached the wagon and was about to peek inside when a bark startled me. An animal scurried around my feet, yipping. It was Duke, Miz Wilma's dog, sniffing, barking, and jumping up to paw my skirt.

I reached down to pet him. "Hey, Duke, remember me."

He sniffed my hand and danced around, yipping.

"Duke." It was Miz Wilma's voice. "What's going on out there?"

I hurried to the tent and bent to pull back the flap. "It's me, Miz Wilma."

"Why, Sam, what took you so long? I've been expecting you."

I laughed on hearing the false name I'd given her when we met and I was pretending to be a boy. "I'm going by my real name now. Today, I'm Cordelia."

She was sitting in a chair, her broken leg, bandaged and splinted from just below her right knee to her ankle, stretched out in front of her.

She flashed me a welcoming smile. "So you are, dear girl. Come sit with me." She gestured toward a three-legged stool. "Tell me about your trip across the plains."

I set my bag on the floor and moved the stool in front of her so we could talk face-to-face. "I came on the Pikes Peak Express. Well over a week of being smashed in a seat."

Miz Wilma grinned and nodded. "I've always said the only way to travel is in your own wagon."

"I'll remember that for next time. For now, I'll settle for a horse or a mule."

A black woman entered the tent. Miz Wilma waved a hand in her direction. "This here is Selma. She's been nursing me back to health in between doing laundry and helping her husband with the cabin."

The husband, a white man considerably older than Selma, came in behind her. Miz Wilma introduced us. "And this is Bart. We met while prospecting. I was trying my hand at panning for gold when I slipped on a rock and tumbled into the creek. Hadn't have been for Bart, I don't know if I could've crawled out."

"Thank goodness, you were there," I said to Bart.

He nodded. "Couldn't let anything happen to the medicine lady."

"Anyway," Miz Wilma continued, "it was while I was prospecting that I met Justin Quinn, that man you've been looking for. We had a bit of a talk about his travels. He's got a scar on the left side of his face. When I saw O'Rourke, I told him to give you the word. I reckon he must've done that since you're here."

"Yes, he did. It took me a while to decide to come. Now that I'm here, where do I find Quinn?"

Bart squatted by the fire and poured coffee into a tin cup. "A place called Sims Gulch."

The name "Sims" stopped me, it being the last name of my three stage companions. "Why is it called that?"

"Sims is the man who made the first discovery of gold, so they named the town after him."

"There's a town?"

Bart grinned. "Depends on what you mean by town."

He paused to sip his coffee, and I remembered Levi saying almost the same thing years ago when we camped at Cottonwood Point, a "town" with three dwellings.

Bart slid to the floor and crossed his legs, resting his cup on his knee. "About a thousand miners spread out along the creek living in tents, lean-tos, wagons, and whatever else they can cobble together for shelter while they pan for gold."

"That many?" How would I ever find Justin Quinn in such a crowd? I went over what I knew about him, about forty years old, red hair, and a long scar down the left side of his face.

He grinned. "There's usually four or five miners to a claim, so it's not as big a place as it sounds. Just ask around. That scar will help you find him. Plus, I understand he's part of the mining committee, so folks will know him."

"What does the mining committee do?"

"Helps keep records of claims and holds court when anyone breaks the laws."

"That sounds impressive, not like I expected."

Miz Wilma chimed in. "It's been a long time. People change."

I reached for her hand. "You haven't. You are as kind as ever. I've missed you—and Duke."

As if on cue, Duke lay down between Miz Wilma's chair and my stool. He turned his brown eyes up at me expectantly.

I scratched behind his ear and patted his head. "I think he remembers me."

"Probably so. What now, Cordelia?"

"I rented a room at the hotel across from the stage station. I reckon tomorrow I'll buy a horse or mule and head for Sims Gulch. Where is it exactly?"

"Just follow Clear Creek. You'll come to it," Miz Wilma said. "But about buying a horse, why don't you use my mules? I'm laid up here for another week or so. That'll probably be enough time for you to tend to business with this Quinn fellow."

I appreciated that she kept my relationship with my father to herself. Having never met him, I didn't want everyone knowing my business and seeing my pain if things went bad.

"Are these the same speedy mules from four years ago?" I asked.

"Now, don't be badmouthing Ready and Waiting. They are sure-footed and will get you where you want to go. And these mountains are no place to try traveling fast. I'm not the only one that's broken a leg or worse from a fall."

"I'll keep that in mind. I appreciate the offer, and I'll be back in the morning to get them. Thank you, Miz Wilma, for all your help. I'd best get back to the hotel now."

Bart got to his feet and brushed his pants. "It's dark out there. I'll walk with you and make sure you get to the hotel okay."

I smiled, relieved at the offer. "Thank you." I nodded at his wife. "Nice to meet you, Selma."

On the way back to the hotel, I looked longingly at the eating house. "It looks closed," I said to Bart. "Do you know if they open for breakfast?"

"They do, and I've heard the food's not bad."

My stomach growled again, but the slices of dried apples in my handbag would have to do until morning.

***

I was up early the next morning. After some consideration of the clothes in my satchel, boy clothes or bloomers, I donned my bloomers, consisting of a pale green dress with a hem that came just below my knees and trousers gathered at the ankle. I tied a straw bonnet with matching green ribbons on my head. My stomach growling, I hurried to the eating house I had spotted the night before. A bell clanged as I stepped through the doorway. Men stared at my clothes, their eyes narrowing in judgement, but I didn't let their looks keep me from having a big breakfast of eggs, potatoes, bacon, and biscuits before heading for Miz Wilma's to collect her two mules, Ready and Waiting. From what I remembered, those names pretty much fit their personalities. Ready was just that while Waiting wanted to stand and think about the road ahead before raising a hoof. Once they both got moving, though, they stayed in step pretty well.

When I arrived at Miz Wilma's, she took one look at me and her eyebrows shot up. "What have you got on, girl?"

"Bloomers," I said. "I figured they would be easier to climb mountains in than a long dress blowing here and there."

"Don't you have any of those boy clothes you used to wear?"

"I do."

"Then given there's about a thousand men to every couple of women in those mountains, you might want to be a boy. Those bloomers will just rile up men wherever you go."

Thinking about the glares I had gotten on my way, I figured she was right. Women were scarce in mining camps, and going as one, particularly wearing the male-aggravating bloomers that signaled a suffragette, would put me in danger. I changed into the clothes Mr. O'Rourke had bought me when I traveled with him: tan wool pants, a matching tan shirt, a dark brown vest and a flat wool cap with a short bill. While the fact that I had not grown much in four years was often a sore point for me, I now appreciated that I could still pass for a boy.

Bart helped me retrieve my trunk from the stage office. Then I repacked my belongings in saddlebags. After more directions from Bart, I was on my way, riding Ready and leading Waiting, who was

67

packed with everything I thought I'd need. I wore sturdy boots and, hearing that mountain nights could be cool, a light jacket borrowed from Miz Wilma. The place known as Sims Gulch was about twenty miles up the canyon, so I would have to camp at least one night alone. I had both a rifle borrowed from Miz Wilma and my derringer for protection and had shortened my name to Cord.

Travel up the canyon was steep and treacherous. Along the way, there were areas dense with tents on the mountain sides and men squatting along the creek, panning for gold every twenty feet or so.

From a distance, they looked the same with their slouch hats, denim or buckskin pants, and cotton shirts. I wondered how I would recognize Justin Quinn when I saw him.

It was on toward evening when someone shouted, "Hey, there. Boy."

The voice sounded familiar. "Sam," he shouted. "Cord. Whoever you are today."

I reined Ready to a stop and looked around.

Coming down the mountain at a trot was a whiskered man in denim pants and a red plaid shirt. I squinted, trying to make out his features, but his beard and mustache made it impossible. I kneed Ready into forward action, but stopped him again when the man skidded to a halt in front of me and grabbed the bridle. "Cord?"

I stared into unforgettable blue eyes. "Max? What are you doing here?"

"Same as everyone else, looking for gold." He leaned to one side, looking around Ready. "I don't see a camera. Does that mean you've given up picture-taking?"

"Some time ago. How did you recognize me?"

"Your clothes. They still look new."

"I haven't had much occasion to wear them. I've been living with my aunt and helping her around the hotel."

"That all worked out, then?"

"Not as I'd hoped, but yes."

"You traveling alone?"

I let out a breath and shook my head. "Do you see anyone with me?"

"No need to be touchy. Just worrying about you. It's getting on toward dark, a dangerous time to travel."

"So what should I do, Max? Or are you going by Max now?"

"Yes, Max Smith. There's hundreds of us Smiths. And you are?"

"Cord."

"No more worries about wanted posters with Cordelia on them?"

"No. That problem was resolved years ago, but yours will never be." Just saying those words caused a flood of sadness in me. One foolish, deadly act would follow Max and anyone who cared for him forever. The lives of a wife or child would be as uncertain as his.

Max made light of his situation. "The great thing about this country is fifty miles from where they want you no one has ever heard of you, particularly if you're a Smith."

"Hmmm." I didn't tell him what he should have known just from the number of times we had met. People moved around. It only took one person who recognized him and wanted the five-hundred-dollar reward to turn him in.

"So come stay the night with me and my partner. You don't want to be wandering around in the dark on these steep cliffs."

He was right. After a day spent picking my way along the drop-offs, I wasn't looking forward to doing that at night, even if we had a good moon. I figured I was as safe with Max as I would be anywhere.

I glanced around at the profusion of tents. "So which one of these grand establishments is yours?"

"Up there," he said, pointing in the direction he had come almost rolling down from. "You think these two old-timers can make it?" He nodded at the mules.

"I reckon they can. They've come this far. Turn loose of the bridle, and we'll see."

He let go and stepped back. I shook the reins and kneed Ready. He took off at a slow walk. When the reins I was holding for Waiting stretched tight, he also began moving. We were soon in Max's camp.

"Where's your partner," I asked.

"Howie will be up soon. It's my turn to fix supper."

I slid off Ready. "I'm glad you're cooking because my campfire skills are rusty."

Max lifted the lid of the pot and stirred the contents with a spoon. "Beans don't take much fixing. Put them in a pot of water and don't let it boil dry." He laid the spoon aside and replaced the lid. "We got hardtack to go with the soup."

I laughed. "What? No fish?"

"There's some trout in the stream, but I haven't caught any yet."

"You'd better have a good aim when you cast a line, or what you'll catch is another miner. How do you all know where to stand?"

"Everyone has a claim, and the claims are a certain size, depending on the kind. The original finders get two claims. The rest, like me and Howie, who are placer mining, get twenty feet along the creek and a hundred up the mountain. We're at the top end of our claim right now. We got stakes out showing where it ends."

"Do you really find gold this way? Does everyone?"

"Not everyone. It's hard work, standing in cold water for hours, swishing around sand and water in the pan. We're making about five dollars a day."

"Not bad money, but it sounds like a lot of work to get it."

"When we get a stake together, we can move on to a new place. Try to be a discoverer instead of someone who comes in after."

"Hey," came a voice from the twilight. "Who's the company?"

"Howie, this is Cord, a friend from Westport. I saw him headed up the trail and chased him down for news of home."

Howie, who looked about my age, dropped down beside me and unlaced his wet boots. "Going anywhere in particular?"

"Looking for family," I said. "A man named Justin Quinn. A friend told my aunt he was out this way and sent me to find him." I glanced at Max. "You know how the West is. Family comes out looking for something and you don't hear from them, they could be dead. You don't know."

Howie got a faraway look in his eye. "Yes, it's easy to lose track of family."

"Sounds like you know something about that," I said.

"I do." He looked down, pulled off his water-soaked socks, and rubbed his feet, red from the cold.

It looked like he didn't want to talk about family, so I turned to Max. "How about your ma and sisters? Are they still in St. Louis?"

Max laughed. "You were right about my mother and that freighter. They got married and he and a nephew are working the farm in between freight runs. And you, Cord. Was your aunt able to help you out?"

I chose my words carefully, seeing as I was passing for a boy. "My ma was too sick to be saved. She died the night we got there. And the baby, too." I closed my eyes, blocking the tears that always threatened at the memory.

"Sorry," Max said. "What did you do after that? I know you didn't get along with your father."

"Aunt Hannah took me and my sisters to Westport. We've been living with her and working in the hotel. But Lucy's thirteen now, and our father sent for her, so I took her back to him." I almost choked on "our father," but without telling more to Howie than I wanted, I had to do it. I decided to change the subject and tease Max. "Not long before that, Mr. O'Rourke stopped by and gave us news about Justin Quinn, so we decided as long as I was heading west, I might as well try to find him."

"The Lothario stopped by? Why's he still hanging around?"

The edge in Max's voice had Howie looking up, raising an eyebrow.

I frowned at Max. He sounded jealous, which was a dumb thing for him to do seeing that I was passing for a boy. "Turns out, he's a friend of my aunt's. For a while, I thought he might become an uncle, but neither of them seems to be of a marrying mind."

Howie wrapped his feet in a buffalo robe and pulled another one over his shoulders. "Grub done yet?"

"Sure thing," Max replied. He spooned beans into a tin plate, put a hard biscuit on the side and handed the meal to Howie. Next he fixed me a plate and one for himself.

We sat around the fire, listening to voices coming up and down the canyon. Before long, we moved into the tent and rolled into our blankets.

***

Howie was a loud snorer. I woke in the cold light of dawn and peeked through the tent flaps. The sun barely streamed through the canyon, a thin shaft hitting the south wall.

Max was stoking the fire, laying on a new log.

I sat, stretched, and pulled the buffalo robe around my shoulders. My jacket was definitely not warm enough for mountain nights. I joined Max at the fire.

"Morning," Max said. "Coffee will be ready soon."

"Thanks. Do you think I'll reach Sims Gulch today?"

"You should. It's about ten more miles up the creek. And folks know Quinn, so finding him shouldn't be a problem. Does your aunt want him to go back east?"

"No, just wants to know what happened to him."

Max shook his head. "Seems like there'd be more to it than that to send you out here by yourself."

Aggravated by his persistence, I snapped, "Well, that's all the story I've got to tell."

"So there is more."

I gritted my teeth. "Like I said."

"Okay." He poured the coffee. "Oatmeal's almost done if you want some."

I lightened up at the mention of food and decided to show some gratitude. "Thanks for feeding me and letting me spend the night."

After we finished eating, he helped me load up the mules.

"Be careful, Cord. There's a lot of good people here, but a lot of bad, too."

"That sounds about like everywhere," I said.

"If you're not staying long, maybe I'll see you on the way down."

"I'll stop by on my way back to see if you're still here. After all, you said you were moving on if you got enough for a grubstake."

As I left the camp, miners were rousing from sleep and some were already heading down the slope toward the creek and another day of panning.

The sun was touching the top of the mountains to the west when I came to a sign that said "Sims Gulch." I was relieved because it would soon be dark. I wandered along the trail through the campsites, looking for someone to ask Quinn's whereabouts.

That's when I heard a ruckus and turned to see Bob, Scott, and Martin Sims. My worst fears about them had been realized. They must be related to the Sims who had discovered the gold here. How was I going to explain dressing as a boy?

I turned up the collar on my jacket, and pulled down the bill of my cap, wishing I was wearing one of those slouch hats with a wide brim. My breath was ragged as I passed a dozen feet or so from them, the area so packed with a crowd of miners there was little room to get by them on the narrow trail.

I guided Ready and Waiting through the milling men, keeping a sideways watch on them. A few feet up the mountain, three men sat around a makeshift table of planks over large stones, a deck of cards in the center. They were scowling at the arguing Sims boys.

Martin stood between Bob and the table of gamblers. "Your father told you to stop betting."

72

"You've had too much to drink, anyway," Scott added, his hand around Bob's forearm.

Bob grabbed his brother by the wrist and pulled Scott's hand off him. Pushing past Martin, Bob shouted, "I'm planning to win back some of my gold."

They were too busy to notice me, so I picked my way around them and kept going.

A quarter of a mile and a couple dozen claims up the creek, I came to a tent with a sign posted on the front that said "Quinn." Remembering that Miz Wilma said my father was some kind of mining court judge, I figured this must be his way of letting folks find him when there was a problem.

I dismounted from Ready and walked up to the closed tent flap. "Hello. Anyone here? Mr. Quinn?"

A man with long gray hair and a weathered face poked his head around the far side of the tent. He looked at me, his forehead wrinkling even more than it was already. "Thought I heard a female voice."

"My voice hasn't changed yet," I said, hoping he'd buy that reason. "I was looking for Mr. Quinn. My aunt sent me to find him."

"Your aunt?"

"She thinks he's related to us."

His eyes twinkled. "Well, I hope she doesn't think we've struck it rich and she's looking to get a share."

I figured he was making a joke. "Nothing like that. She just wondered where he'd got to. It's been a number of years."

He harrumphed and his eyes narrowed. "I reckon it has. I knowed him at least ten of those years, and you're the first to come looking." He nodded. "He's straight on down the mountain, panning for gold."

"Mind if I tie my mules here."

"Go ahead."

I secured the mules to a bush and headed down the mountain toward the father I'd traveled six hundred miles to meet.

13) BAKING PIES

Lucy

Pa drove us to the church pie sale in his buggy. He'd made the wheels and the frame himself and stretched a black canvas across the top. It was a two-seater, and I had the back seat, with baskets containing my dishcloth-covered contest pies, along with fried chicken and green beans for the community dinner in a crate on the floor next to my feet.

Pa stopped our buggy in a line with one other buggy and several buckboards and set the brake. "Help your sister down," he said to Ambrose.

Ambrose leaped to the ground and came around to help me, catching me at the waist with both hands, lifting me off the buggy, and setting me on the ground. "I'll get the food baskets for you," he said.

We walked to a white canvas tent where temporary tables made of planks across sawhorses and topped with white tablecloths were set up. Several people milled about, chatting. Four men were playing horseshoes off to one side.

Mrs. Collins greeted me. "Lucy, I see you've come to show off your baking talent. Write your name on these papers, one for the tasting contest and one for the bake sale."

I did as she said and positioned the pies in the places indicated. Then I set the chicken and green beans on the covered dish table. Ambrose took the crate back to the buggy.

I took a look around, something I'd been too nervous to do last Sunday. The church, a one-story white wood building, looked brand-new, and I said as much to Mrs. Collins.

"Finished it about six months ago. Before that, we held services in Reverend Sherwood's parlor or outside on the grass when the weather was good."

Pa showed up then with a man who looked to be about thirty years old. The man's eyes lit up when he saw me.

"There she is," Pa said to his friend, like he was bursting with pride. "My daughter, Lucy." He put his hand on my back. "Lucy, say hello to George Chapman. He's come over from Ft. Riley just for the sale, a bachelor in need of a homemade pie. Isn't that right, George?"

"Indeed, it is." He held out his hand. "It's nice to meet you, Miss Pierce."

I held out my hand, expecting to shake, but he took hold of my fingers and raised them to his lips, letting them brush the top of my hand.

Flustered, I managed a "pleased-to-meet-you" in return.

I stood, my blue calico skirt over six petticoats worn for the occasion swaying in the light breeze, a tight smile on my face, with the men looking at me expectantly, like I was supposed to say something more, but I hadn't a notion what that might be.

Finally, Pa broke the silence. "George teaches school at the fort."

"Oh," I said, my smile a little brighter. "Perhaps you know a teacher for our school here in Hidden Springs. My little sisters may be coming here to live soon. They're seven and nine, and they love school, but my brother, Ambrose, told me our last teacher married, so we need one."

"I will keep that in mind when I write to my friends in the east," Mr. Chapman said.

Reverend Sherwood rang a bell. "It's time for the picnic. Let's bow our heads in prayer and give thanks for the food and the beautiful day. When we're finished eating, we'll have the baking contest and pie sale."

After Reverend Sherwood said a brief blessing, we grabbed tin plates and got in line. About thirty people had turned out. Everything looked delicious. I hoped the green beans and fried chicken I'd brought would taste as good as they had looked when I fixed them.

"Lucy, there you are." Susan called from a few feet away. She walked toward me, talking. "I just saw your pies. They look perfect."

"Thank you, Susan." I gestured toward my new acquaintance. "This is Mr. Chapman. He teaches school at Ft. Riley."

"Mr. Chapman," Susan greeted him with a nod and a smile, her warm brown eyes signaling a friendly nature I hadn't managed to show him.

"Miss?"

"Miss Hogan," she said.

Mr. Chapman seemed flustered. He held his greeting hand at his side, opening and closing it like he wanted to do something but wasn't sure he should. I figured he wanted to do the hand kiss thing again and wondered why he didn't just go ahead.

He glanced at Pa, so I did, too. Pa was all scowls, his mouth a thin line and eyes glaring at Susan.

Susan glanced at him and then squeezed my hand. "When the judging is about to start, you need to come and stand behind your pie."

"Okay."

She left to join the line with Willy and the rest of her family.

We went through the line and joined Mayor Tompkins at a table where he was saving seats for us. Pa immediately began talking city business with him, leaving me to entertain Mr. Chapman. My previous conversations with teachers had been as their student, so finding common ground beyond the nice day we were having proved difficult. Ambrose came to my rescue by talking about the school building at the fort and comparing it to our school in Hidden Springs. After the meal was over, Susan was back, urging me to join her. I turned to Mr. Chapman. "Please excuse me."

"Of course," he said.

"Pa?"

"Go along, but I want a word with you later."

"Yes, Pa." With Susan tugging my hand, we scurried across the lawn to the tent.

Inside, I found my pie next to Susan's and quickly took my place behind it. There were eight pies for judging. Standing in a huddle at the far end of the table were four men and two women, each armed with a plate, a fork, and a cup of water.

Reverend Sherwood rang a hand bell, and everyone got quiet.

"Thank you all for coming out on this fine June day to support the church and our need for new hymnals. Eight of the finest pies I have ever seen are lined up, and behind them are the talented cooks who brought them into being. We thank God for their talents and their generosity."

He waved his hand, gesturing at the judges. "Here are the lucky folks who get the first tastes: Mrs. Collins, who runs our fine boardinghouse and is one of the best cooks in these parts; Doc Sloan, who certainly knows good food when he sees it; Elspeth Ward, another fine cook and mother of eight boys, and bachelor farmers Ed Crow, Jim Chase, and Harley Wilkes, who are always looking for a good pie and the cook who baked it."

There was general laughter among the listeners.

"So pastry makers, divide your pies in half. Then divide that half into six pieces, one for each of our judges. Judges move down the line and collect your samples. Ladies first."

I was last in line, so I could see all the pies that had been entered: strawberry, blueberry, pumpkin, custard, and three apple. I added my slice of peach to a judge's plate and sneaked a look at Susan. She grinned at me. Ours had the best looking crusts.

The judges carried their samples to a table and began the tasting. We bakers stood behind our pies and fidgeted. Indistinct chatter came from the table. Then the judges pushed their plates aside, each dish still containing tiny morsels, and bent over papers, marking their favorites. Then there was more discussion and counting, pointing at various morsels, and more note taking on the papers. At last, Doc Sloan motioned for Reverend Sherwood to join them.

After more consultation with the judges, Reverend Sherwood made a final list and again rang the bell for the crowd's attention.

"Folks, the judges were split on a winner. After much discussion, we decided on a tie. The first place winners are Miss Susan Hogan, whose pies are frequent prizewinners, and Miss Lucy Pierce, who has come home after a long stay in Westport with family. Second place goes to the strawberry pie and third to the pumpkin. The judges say all the pies are excellent. Our bakers will slice tiny tastes so you can line up with plates and taste the ones you may want to buy."

While everyone was grabbing plates, Susan showed me how to cut the remaining half of the pie into bite-sized squares. Even so, there didn't look like enough to go around as folks gathered for their samples, most of them men of various ages and dress. In fact, some had arrived after the picnic, wearing uniforms, so they must have come over from Ft. Riley just for the pie. Well, maybe it was for more than the pie because some lingered at the end of the table, trying to talk to Susan and me, flirting. I was enjoying the attention until I saw Pa giving me some dark looks.

And then it was time for the auction. According to the rules, if the person who won the bid wished her to, the cook would share a piece with him or her. Of course, those folks bidding were mostly single men who didn't have a cook at home and wanted a good dessert, good company, or both.

With Susan's pie placing first, hers was the first to be auctioned, bids starting at twenty-five cents. The bids came fast and furious, shooting to two dollars before slowing down a bit. At four dollars, bidding dropped off to two determined men: Mr. Chapman and a soldier. When the bid reached five dollars, Reverend Sherwood called for five dollars and twenty-five cents. There was a moment's quiet, and I thought the soldier won, but then Mr. Chapman signaled his bid and won. He was standing beside Pa, and Pa looked like he was about to burst, his face all red and his lips set in that frown of displeasure I was coming to dread.

That's when I realized he'd considered Mr. Chapman a possible beau for me. A teacher must have seemed like a good catch since he was well-educated. I wondered about his family.

But then it was time to auction my pie since I had tied for first. As with the bidding for Susan's pastry, it started at a brisk pace. Willy even bid, just like he promised, but when the bidding went over two dollars, he dropped out. The last bidder said five dollars, the reverend said "sold" and I and my pie were collected by a soldier.

We joined Susan and Mr. Chapman and settled down on a blanket spread under an elm tree to enjoy dessert while the auction continued.

Pa had lost interest in the bidding and headed for his buggy with two other men, pointing at the frame and wheels, obviously showing off his blacksmithing skills, maybe trying for orders. Pa never wasted any time, but took advantage of every event to bring in business.

I had always been proud of his ambition to be the best, to have the best, but now that he seemed focused on finding his idea of the best person for me to marry, that pride was dwindling. I wanted my own choice in my own time. And although the soldier who purchased my pie wasn't even in the running for being my beau, he was handsome and fun to talk to on a glorious afternoon in June.

***

Pa stared straight ahead as he drove us home. He didn't speak to me at all and said only a couple of words to Ambrose about chores.

Ambrose tried to help me with a compliment. "Tied for first. That's good for your first cooking contest."

"Susan gave me some advice about the crust and filling," I said, wanting to make Pa aware that she was a good person.

Pa didn't react the way I expected. "I told you to stay away from that Hogan tart. What is it going to take for you to obey me like God says you should."

Without thinking, I snapped, "The Bible also says you should love your neighbor, and Susan and her family are our neighbors."

Pa stopped the buggy, dismounted, reached up, and grabbed my wrist. "You will not disrespect me. Not in your actions and not in your words." He jerked me out of the wagon. "Walk home, do your chores, and go to your room. From now on, you will leave the house only for church, and I will drive you there. You will not have visitors. Do not answer the door when I am gone. Do you understand?"

"How long will I be confined to the house?"

"Until you learn to do as I say. Given the way you've acted so far, that may be until you get married. I'm waiting for an answer. Do you understand?"

"Yes, Pa."

"Start walking. And no stops along the way."

"Yes, Pa."

"I'll be waiting for you on the front steps. See that you arrive in a reasonable time."

"Yes, Pa."

He climbed onto the buggy, cracked the whip, and left me in the dust.

Thoroughly defeated, I plodded toward home. When I passed the Hogan place, I was glad they were still at the church. Susan or Willy would have tried to talk to me. What would I have done? I couldn't just stick my nose in the air and walk on. Susan was a friend, the only one I had here, and now I couldn't talk to her.

I trudged on, thinking about all the warnings Cordelia and Aunt Hannah had given me. One of the last things Aunt Hannah had said before I boarded the stage to Hidden Springs was that I could come back to her if things didn't work out.

But Pa would never let me go. He had a picture in his mind of me married to some powerful, rich man, and when Pa got a picture in his mind, he worked until he got it in real life.

Our circle drive was in sight, the stone house cold and empty of love, Pa on the front step staring down the road, something in his hand. As I came closer, I realized it was his pocket watch. He was timing me.

I was in prison, and I had put myself there.

***

The next day was Sunday. Church was over, the noon meal cooked, eaten, and cleaned up after, and it was time to write to Ella and Jennie. I tried the kitchen table in the new house, but nothing came. I glanced out the window at our old cabin, and it seemed like the place to write to my little sisters, the place we had all called home together.

A light breeze cooled me as I stepped outside, pen and paper in hand and a match in my pocket along with Ma's comb, the one I had found in the crack between the floor and the wall. I knew in spite of the breeze that the cabin would be hot inside. I glanced around. Ambrose was working in a lean-to, sanding a piece of wood. He was always making something, whether it be of stone or wood or metal. For a boy of fourteen, his abilities were amazing. Mine, on the other hand, were lacking.

Sunday was supposed to be a day of rest, but I found it almost as busy as any other day. I was up just as early as on the weekdays, cooking breakfast and clearing the dishes. I wasn't sure that attending church could truly be called rest since I had learned through Pa's lectures that I must be on my best behavior in public. I must look beautiful and dutiful, capable and smart. I must at all times look like excellent wife material for those my father deemed "good enough" for me. Just thinking about all those demands made me tired. Pa was even now at his desk in the otherwise empty library going over receipts, making plans, reading newspapers, looking for ways to build his wealth and influence in the territory.

I entered the cabin and left the door open to catch the breeze. When I had been here before, I had seen a candle on the table, so today I had brought a match from the house. After lighting the candle, I slid onto the bench and placed my letter paper on the table. I pulled the faux tortoise shell comb from my pocket, turning it over, studying the scrolls of tiny rhinestone chips that curved up the back. Ma had worn it only once—to a Christmas ball when we lived in Westport and Pa worked at his family's blacksmith shop.

Strange how Pa, who was so dedicated to being an important citizen now, had spent so little time socializing then. Too bad Ma hadn't had more social opportunities to wear the comb. I laid it aside and picked up the pen. Clutching it tightly between my fingers, I dipped the pen into the bottle of ink on the table and began to write.

> Dear Ella and Jennie,
> I have been home almost two weeks, and it has been a busy time. Ambrose has been patient in helping me adjust to my routine of chores. He is the best big brother ever, and I can hardly wait until we are all together.
> That may be longer than I thought because the house isn't really finished, at least not inside. It needs paper for the walls, rugs for the floors, and furniture. I get to choose those things. It is a big responsibility.

I lay the pen down, realizing I'd written almost the same thing the previous week. I picked up Ma's comb, rubbing the back, trying to find something new and positive to write when Pa's voice roared.

"Lucy! Where are you? You better be out here. I find you've gone off somewhere, I'll—"

Ambrose's voice cut in, lower, so I couldn't hear what he was saying.

I shut my eyes and tried to stop shaking.

In seconds, Pa was standing in the cabin door, glowering at me. "We got a perfectly good table in the house for writing. Better light, too." He stomped across the space between the door and the table and grabbed my hand. "Where did you get this comb? It was your Ma's. Did that witch Hannah run off with it when your Ma died?"

"No, I found it last week near where her bed used to be. It must have fallen into the crack between the floorboard and wall the day those slave hunters smashed everything. We never saw it after that. Ma was so upset. Remember?"

Ambrose followed Pa into the cabin and stood a bit behind. "I remember," he said. "She thought they stole it."

"Humph." Pa snatched the comb from my hand. "I want to know when you leave the house. I want to know where you're going. There won't be any more spending time with those Hogan brats."

"Yes, Pa."

He stomped out, taking Ma's comb with him.

Ambrose took a seat on the bench across from me. "Are you okay?"

I drew in a deep breath and let it go. "Yes. It's just nothing is like I'd dreamed it would be."

He toyed with the ink bottle. "That's probably my fault. I should have reminded you how controlling Pa is."

"I wouldn't have believed you. Aunt Hannah and Cordelia tried to tell me, but I refused to listen to them. I was in my own world of daydreams." I looked at my letter. "What should I tell Ella and Jennie? They believed every word I said."

Ambrose shook his head. "Tell them you love them."

Gripping the pen, I finished the letter to my sisters and gave it to Ambrose to mail. I wasn't going anywhere for who knew how long. I fell asleep that night, clutching the locket with Ma's hair in it, wishing Pa hadn't taken her comb. What was it to Pa that he had to take it from me?

I awoke the next morning and went through the morning routine of gathering eggs, cooking breakfast, cleaning up the dishes, milking the cow, and feeding the livestock. My next chore was churning butter. I carried the wooden cream-filled churn outside to a worktable in the shade, thankful I only had to crank a handle until the butter came instead of shaking a jar.

While I worked, I stared at the cabin and thought of Ma. Now I knew why she had agreed to send us girls to Aunt Hannah's. It really was best for us. Why hadn't I been able to I see that? But truly, I didn't remember Pa being as bad as he was now. Maybe Ma's death had done this to him.

Whatever caused it, I didn't know what to do. Pa wouldn't want Ella to come until she was my age, so she was safe for four years. What could I do to save her from my fate?

"Hey, there. Don't you ever answer your door?"

It was Willy, fishing pole in hand.

"I'm not allowed to," I said.

"Not allowed to answer the door?"

I nodded. "I'm not allowed to talk to you or your sister either."

"Oh." He propped the pole against the side of the house. "Why's that?"

"Because you don't fit Pa's list of qualities my future husband should have. He doesn't want anyone getting the wrong idea about us. It might hurt my marriage prospects."

"Oh."

"'Oh!' Is that all you have to say?"

He blinked. "I came to tell you I'm sorry I didn't have enough money to buy your pie and you had to eat with that old soldier from the fort. But I guess your father was probably happy about that."

"That you didn't have the winning bid, yes. That the soldier won, no. He wanted that teacher to win, but Mr. Chapman bought Susan's pie instead. I wonder if he understood he was being introduced to me as a possible marriage partner."

"Wow."

"So you know two words."

Willy chuckled. "Ma says I was slow learning to talk."

"Don't be slow learning to listen. You'd better leave. If Pa comes home and finds you here, I don't like to think what he might do."

Willy picked up his fishing pole. "Okay. Are we friends even if I can't stop by?"

"Yes. And tell Susan the same. I don't want her thinking bad of me when I don't speak."

"I'll tell her." He gave a slight wave before disappearing around the corner of the house.

I lifted the lid of the churn. Yellow flecks of butter were forming. At least, I had learned to make butter during my four years in Westport.

***

Supper was over, the cow milked, all the chores done, and it was still light. I went into the library where Pa was working on business records, Ambrose following me. I knocked at the open door. When Pa looked up, I said, "I want to visit Ma's grave."

Pa frowned. "I told you that you weren't leaving this farm."

"But I want to put flowers on Ma's grave. What will people say? I've been here two weeks and haven't gone to see her grave."

I had him stumped. Looking good mattered. He stared at me.

Ambrose spoke up. "I can take her, Pa"

"Well." He settled back in his chair. "Straight there and straight back. No lollygagging."

"Yes, sir," Ambrose said.

Pa squinted at Ambrose. "I'm depending on you to keep this one in line."

"Yes, sir."

He waved us away. "Go on then. See you're back before dark."

"Thank you," I said, backing away from the doorway.

We hurried down the hall to the kitchen. I took off my apron and hung it on a peg before rushing out the back door and around the house to the road. As we walked toward the cemetery, we stepped to the side now and then to pick wildflowers, purple and yellow and white. They made a nice bouquet. I'd brought crochet yarn to tie around the stems.

I looked straight ahead when we reached the Hogan place, feeling strange. "Susan was so nice to me," I said. "She helped me figure out how to thicken the pie filling and make a better crust, and I have to stick up my nose and not talk to her."

"I'm sure she understands," Ambrose said.

I looked sideways at him. "Is Pa going to pick someone for you to marry?"

His lips pressed tight for a moment. "He thinks he is."

"How will you stop him?"

His hands clenched. "When the time comes, I will say no. Until then, I won't argue about it."

"I probably don't have very long. He was introducing me to a prospective bridegroom at the pie contest." My hand tightened on the flower stems. "Why is he in such a hurry to get me married?"

"He's afraid you'll fall for some worthless boy like Willy and end up like Ma, with a baby on the way and no husband. He figures he'll have a hard time finding someone who'll take you if that happens."

I frowned. "You believe Willy is worthless?"

"It doesn't matter what I believe. Pa says he is."

I sighed. "I wonder if Cordelia will find her pa, and if she does, if she'll be as disappointed in him as I am in ours."

We came to the cemetery. There were at least a couple dozen graves. I remembered six counting Ma's when we buried her.

"The town and the cemetery are growing," I said as we picked our way around a row of graves and stopped in front of Ma's. There were two headstones: one for Mark who had lived only a week and one for Ma and the stillborn baby buried with her. Kneeling in the grass, I laid the flowers on her grave and studied the writing on the stone: Minerva True Pierce, beloved wife and mother, and her infant son.

"I chiseled the words," Ambrose said. "She was a good mother, but she was always sick."

"She was always in the family way," I said, "and then she died." That seemed to sum up the whole story of her life.

Ambrose knelt beside me. "She always told me what a good job I did after I finished the chores. She said I should remember to tell you the same when you did something because Pa didn't say enough good things to us." He pulled a weed by the stone. "She wanted us all to play more when we were little, but there was always too much work to do."

"I guess you didn't play much while I was gone."

"No time—and no one to play with if there'd been time. It's why I wanted you back, Lucy. I missed you, missed times like now when we talked. But that was selfish. Now you're here, and Pa won't let up until he finds someone for you to marry. Maybe if you quit fighting with him, he'll slow down on the marriage idea until Ella is old enough to come and run the house. He wants you to marry well, but he wants someone around to take care of all the woman chores, too."

I picked a blade of grass and twisted it around my finger. "I thought I'd be good at those 'woman chores,' but it turns out I'm awful at them. And I never imagined I would be so completely alone, that I wouldn't be allowed to be friends with our neighbors."

"I know it's hard. I like Susan and Willy, too, but if you don't want to be married before Christmas, you'd better concentrate on being the best housekeeper possible and doing exactly what Pa wants. The more he's riled, the quicker you're going to end up with a wedding ring on your finger."

"But I can't keep that up forever. Like you said, in four years, Ella will be old enough to take over. Then I will have to say 'yes' to marrying someone."

"You'll be older. Maybe you can leave then."

"You think he will ever let me go?" I was being a pest, but I couldn't help asking him once more. "What about you, Ambrose? Are you going to let him choose a wife for you?"

His fists were clenching again. "No. When that time comes, we will have a big fight."

"Ma wouldn't want any of this to happen."

"But Ma's not here. Even if she was, he wouldn't pay much attention to her opinions. He never did. It's all up to us."

14) ACQUAINTANCES

Cordelia

The man I'd been searching for was only a hundred yards away, squatting in a stream down the mountain from me, panning for gold. I picked my way down the rough terrain, stones shifting beneath my feet, making me glad I was dressed as a boy. Trousers would protect my limbs if I should fall, and I didn't have to worry about a skirt flying up.

A rock dislodged and rolled, clattering its way downhill. The man's shoulders bunched. He laid the pan aside and reached for something in his left boot. "Who's there?" he shouted.

"Are you Justin Quinn?" I called out, continuing toward him.

"Who wants to know?" He shifted on the balls of his feet, twisting his neck to see me.

His question aggravated me. Why didn't he just answer? "I do. I've been told he's my father. Are you him?"

He stood and tilted his head to one side. "I'm Quinn. Don't know about the father part? Who said so?"

"My mother. Minerva True. Remember her?" I was within a dozen feet of him, watching his face, trying to read what he was thinking. He didn't look surprised, but he didn't look happy either.

"I remember hearing she was married to some blacksmith and they had a baby. Heard it was a girl."

I stopped no more than four feet from him. I'd always wondered what I'd do if I ever got this close. Part of me wanted to scream my anger and pain at him and push him off balance into the stream. If I was lucky, he'd hit his head on a rock and die. But part of me wanted him to somehow make it okay that in seventeen years he'd never come looking for me.

"Did my Aunt Hannah tell you that?"

"Yes, it was Hannah who told me the baby was a girl." He took off his hat and used his shirt sleeve to wipe sweat from his forehead. "I'm still working on the father part."

The motion pushed shaggy red hair away from his face, and I saw the scar Aunt Hannah had told me ran down his left cheek from just in front of his ear to his neck. I clenched my fists, and my vision blurred as anger welled in me. "Aunt Hannah said you could have figured out the baby Ma had was yours if you'd wanted to."

His chin came up, and he clamped the hat on his head. "Seemed to me the child had a good life that didn't include me. It was best to leave it be, boy or girl."

Inwardly trembling, I fought to hold back tears while I searched for the words to tell him what that "good life" had really been when the gray-haired man who had pointed me down here shouted from the pine trees above.

"Justin. We got trouble."

The man who had not yet admitted to being my father grabbed my arm as he passed me and towed me up the mountain after him.

"What is it, Coop?" he asked when we reached the trail that ran through the canyon. We heard shouting in the distance and then a gunshot.

Coop jerked his head at the sound. "I told you that youngest Sims boy was going to be trouble. He done gambled away a claim that was his father's, and, of course, his old man doesn't want to let go. Old Jules is pissed, and I reckon that was his gun that just went off. We'd best get on down there before someone gets killed."

Shaking his head, Justin Quinn strode off in the direction of trouble, and I followed.

A crowd had gathered with Bob Sims and an older man I took to be his father in the center, along with a small, gray-whiskered miner faced off with them, his pistol in his hand. Scott and Martin were off to the side, their hands on their guns.

"Here's Quinn now," one of the men in the crowd shouted.

The gray-whiskered miner looked up, relief in his eyes when he saw the man I believed to be my father. Jerking his head in Quinn's direction, he said, "Here's the mining-district judge. Let's hear what he's got to say." He holstered his pistol.

Quinn joined the Sims bunch and the angry miner inside the ring of onlookers. "Jules, it looks like you're the one who feels wronged. What happened?"

"This young fellow horns in on our game, wanting to gamble, so we dealt out some cards. Come along several hands and he lost his poke of gold, so he said he'd bet his claim. I put up my claim to be fair. Well, he lost, and come to find out, he don't have the paperwork for it. The mine belongs to his daddy. That would be Sims here." Jules pointed to a big man with cold, gray eyes, "and he's not letting go. We know what happens to someone who don't pay their bets." He patted the pistol at his side.

Quinn's eyes narrowed as he studied Bob Sims. "What about it? Is Jules telling the truth?"

Bob's face was sour. "It's about right."

"Only about? What's wrong with it?"

Bob hung his head and didn't speak.

Instead, his father took a step toward Jules and offered his opinion. "What's wrong is the boy was taken advantage of by this old coot."

Jules drew himself up stiff and proud. "You saying I cheated your kid?"

Mr. Sims took another step toward Jules, hands on hips, towering over the older man. "I'm saying you saw he was young and took advantage of him."

Jules didn't give ground. "If the boy's old enough to come looking for a card game and put up a bet, he's old enough to pay off."

Quinn said, "That sounds about right to me. Since this boy doesn't own what he bet, how can we settle it? What sounds right to you, Jules?"

"His daddy should pay up for him."

Mr. Sims responded with a scornful laugh. "You can't expect me to give over a rich claim like that because my son acted stupid."

All around men grumbled, shifting and nudging each other, faces scowling, fists clenching like they might throw a few punches or worse.

"Sounds like the jury's not happy with that answer," Quinn said. "Maybe we should find something that would satisfy Jules. You got anything in mind besides the claim, Jules?"

"He could pay me off in gold dust."

"How much?" Mr. Sims asked.

The question seemed to settle down the group of miners that was gathered around doing the work a jury would if there was one.

Jules scrunched his face in thought. "Well, now. You've been bragging it's probably worth fifty thousand or more, but I reckon I only won, let's see, how much would the boy own? There's him and you and the other boy. Then there's the nephew. Well, I guess about a fifth. Then I don't have to work to get it out of the ground, so I'd say five thousand sounds about right."

Quinn turned to Mr. Sims, whose face flushed a dark red. "I'd say two thousand."

"Want to make that three and we have a deal and your boy is off the hook," Jules countered.

Mr. Sims nodded. "Three it is. Quinn, bring a scale and we'll measure it out."

"Come down to my tent with the gold. We'll weigh it there." Quinn turned to Bob. "I hope you learned something from this, boy. Don't bet what's not yours."

Bob glared at Quinn, venom in his eyes, but he kept his mouth shut.

The ring of men began to break up. However, as we headed for Quinn's tent, Jules and Coop walking side by side, several of the miners trotted along with us.

We stood around, waiting until and Mr. Sims and Bob showed up about thirty minutes later with four pokes of gold. I reckoned that Bob had been getting an earful of criticism from his father because his head was down while Quinn measured the yellow metal dust and small nuggets in batches and kept a tally, scraping the weighed gold into a new poke. It took three of the bags stuffed full to come to three thousand dollars. When Quinn finished his calculations and handed the bags to Jules, Mr. Sims said real loud, "Be on notice. Anyone else gambles with my son gets nothing from me. You'll have to take it out of his hide—and he won't have much of that left after I'm done with him tonight."

He gave Bob a shove toward the trail.

Within minutes, everyone but Coop, Jules, I, and my father had gone.

Jules stuck out a hand. "Thanks, Quinn. That could have gotten ugly without you."

"Your problems are just beginning, Jules. Everyone knows you got that gold. Watch out or somebody will hit you over the head for it."

Jules nodded. "Reckon I should get my partners and light out for Denver. Got enough here for a grubstake to find my own mother lode."

Coop glanced at Quinn and me. "I'll walk you to your camp, Jules."

"Thanks, Coop. I appreciate that."

The two men left Quinn and me facing each other and me trying to think what to say.

Quinn reached over, removed the cap from my head and pulled the pin that held my hair in a bun.

Once again, I had failed to fool someone into believing I was a boy. "When did you guess?" I asked.

"About the same time Coop gave us a holler to come solve the scuffle between Jules and the Sims bunch." He handed back my hat and hairpin. "Put your hair up and put this back on. Staying a boy seems like a good idea when there's probably not more than three women in this gulch and none of them respectable." He squatted beside the fire, stoked it, and chucked in another log. "So why'd you come?"

My hands shook as I twisted my hair in a bun, and my voice was as shaky as my hands when I answered. "To see who you are, what kind of person. To ask why you didn't love my mother enough to care about what happened to her."

He glanced at me. "How is your mother?"

"Dead."

He dropped the stick he'd been poking the fire with and his eyes rounded. "When did that happen?"

"Four years ago. Died having a baby—her tenth. Too weak from all the others to live."

The flames were shooting up now.

"And the child?"

"He died, too."

"Do you have many brothers and sisters?"

"Three half-sisters and a half-brother living—that I know of." This was crazy. I had come to get answers from him, and he was asking all the questions. "What about you? Do I have more half-brothers and sisters from you?"

He frowned, his forehead wrinkling. "No."

"Does that 'no' mean absolutely not—or not that you know of?"

He picked up the stick and poked at the fire again. "Not that I know of, but I'm pretty sure of no."

I pulled my cap on. "How can parents just go off and leave their children without another thought?"

He stopped poking the fire and stared into it. "How, indeed?"

There was such sadness in his voice, that I took a closer look. "Well, you did it. Why?"

He turned from the fire and sat as though mesmerized by something on the mountain beyond us. I had almost given up on getting an answer when he said, "Because I wasn't sure you were mine. Minerva married right away. You could have been her husband's child."

I shook my head. "Even Hiram knew better than that. So did everyone in the family, and not a single one of them ever let me forget it."

There was misery in his eyes when he looked at me. "I'm sorry. I figured you'd have a better life if I stayed away."

Unable to contain my rage, I paced the camp, small as it was, turning and whirling, the pain gushing from my mouth like blood from a deep wound. "Some better life, to get called a bastard, a slut, to work from sunup to sundown taking care of the house and garden and scrubbing and cleaning by the age of nine. To be told everything I did was wrong, that I was too stupid to do anything right. It would have been really hard for you to do better than that." I stopped for breath, glaring at him, waiting for what he would say.

He studied his boots and was silent.

"Say something," I demanded.

"I've said I was sorry." He folded his arms across his chest. "What else can I say?"

I stopped pacing and glared at him. "Tell me why?"

"I was young and dumb." He touched the scar on his face. "Did your Aunt Hannah tell you how I got this?"

"Gambling. A fight over money."

"Yes, like young Bob Sims this evening, I got into a game that didn't go well for me. Unlike him, I was sure the winner had cheated. When I confronted him, we fought, and I got this scar on my face. I had lost all the money I meant to spend on a new life with Minerva, and I had no prospects. How could I ask Minerva to come with me when I had nothing to give her, nothing for us to live on? By the time I thought I might have a chance, it was too late." He shook his head. "That's all there is."

"Didn't you ever want to see me, to make sure if I was yours and how I was?"

"No."

"That's it? Just 'no'?"

"That's it."

It was my time to be quiet and stare at the fire.

After a couple of minutes, he said, "I'll take care of your mules. Do you need anything from your packs?"

"I have a bedroll."

He nodded and disappeared into the night. I heard him working with the mules. I turned the bill of my cap down and sat gazing at the mountainside. The canyon was alive with campfires, but my heart was dark, the flame of hope that had flickered there for a father had been extinguished.

Coop tromped into camp, removed a lid from a kettle at the edge of the fire, and stirred the contents. "Got rabbit stew here, boy. Want to try some?"

So Quinn hadn't told him I was a girl. "Sure, why not? Name's Cord, by the way."

"Good to meet you, Cord." He picked up a tin plate and spooned stew into it. "Never did say why you wanted to speak to Justin."

"He's my father."

Coop nodded as he handed me the plate. "I thought as much, just the way things were going. You don't look like it went the way you wanted."

I shook my head. "I was a stupid kid to think he had any feeling for me. I guess I already knew, but I had to travel all this way to be sure."

"He's a hard man to get close to." He filled a plate for himself.

"You seem to have managed."

93

"Only took ten years of working at it." He raised an eyebrow. "You planning to spend that kind of time?"

"I'll be on my way back to Westport tomorrow morning."

Coop set his plate on a nail keg. He hunkered down beside it, scooped up a spoonful of stew and blew on it. "Sounds best."

Quinn joined us, carrying my bedroll. I had begun thinking of him by his last name during the trial, and it seemed the right way to do it. He wasn't really a father and didn't want to be.

"What 'sounds best'?" he asked.

Coop said, "Young Cord here says he's leaving tomorrow."

Quinn nodded. "Sounds like a good idea." He cast me a sideways glance. "Guess you should turn in if you want to get an early start."

***

I awoke before sunup. Quinn had already built up the fire and made coffee. After a quick cup and a flapjack, I was on my way.

I was almost out of the cluster of ramshackle cabins and tents that made up Sims Gulch when Bob Sims stumbled into my path, whisky bottle in hand.

"Hey! You were that kid with Quinn last night. Who does he think he is, butting into a man's business?"

"He thinks he's the man elected by the miners to solve disputes." I nudged Ready with my knees and pulled the reins to go around Bob, but he grabbed Ready's bridle.

"Hold up there. I know that voice, and it ain't no boy's."

Ready was stomping around now, making a high-pitched "h-e-e-e-e" sound. Bob grabbed my arm and tugged. I pulled back.

Martin and Scott came running. "What's going on, Bob? Let go of that boy."

Bob laughed. "This ain't no boy." He swung his arm up and hit the brim of my cap with his hand.

The hat fell off, the hairpin dislodged, and the bun came loose. My hair cascaded around my shoulders.

Bob snarled at me. "It's Miss Proper Pierce from the stagecoach all done up like a boy. Why's that, Miss Pierce?"

He spat out. "Miss Pierce" like it was some dirty thing to be.

"To keep away men like you who don't know how to behave around a lady," I said.

Bob snorted. "Don't see no lady here. Just some fool female decked out in boy's clothes."

Martin had disappeared, leaving Scott to calm his brother.

"Let go of her, Bob. Father's already mad enough about last night. Don't make it worse."

"What's she doing here, anyway?" Bob turned on me, jerking my arm again. "What are you doing here?"

I pulled back. "Just what I said on the stage, looking for a long-lost family member, and I found him. Not that it's any of your business."

"She's right," Scott said. "Let her go."

A crowd gathered, something I was thankful for unless the men turned against me—a woman in boy's clothing.

"I found Quinn. I talked to him and learned enough to satisfy my aunt's curiosity. Now I want to leave. Let go so I can pass."

The explosion of a gunshot echoed through the canyon.

Quinn pointed a pistol at Bob. "Take your hands off my niece, Sims, or I'll aim the next shot at your knee."

Bob's father pushed his way through the crowd. "What's going on here?"

"Your son is assaulting my niece. He needs to step aside and let her pass."

"Dammit, Bob, can't I let you out of my sight for a minute?" Mr. Sims came up behind Bob, grabbed the back of his neck and squeezed. "Let go of her."

Bob bunched up his shoulders and released me.

Mr. Sims jerked him out of my path and shoved him. Bob stumbled and shouted, "This ain't over."

Quinn turned to Coop. "I'll be taking Cordelia down the mountain. I'm appointing you judge while I'm gone."

Coop nodded.

"As long as I'm going to Denver, I may as well pick up supplies," Quinn said. "Stay here with Cordelia while I get my mule."

"Will do." Coop picked up my cap and handed it to me. "You want to climb down to wait."

"I'll stay here. Quinn shouldn't be long."

Quinn was back about twenty minutes later. We headed down the mountain with him in the lead, single file in narrow places, side by side when the trail allowed.

We didn't talk for a while. It seemed to me we'd said it all the night before. He didn't want family. That was the end of it. He'd come to my rescue, but that could be put down to his being what amounted to the law in Sims Gulch. Still, appreciation was in order.

Keeping my voice flat, I said, "Thanks for making Bob back off."

"Just doing my job," he replied with an equal lack of emotion.

My hands tightened on the reins. When I wanted to, I was as good at not showing my feelings as anyone I knew. "That's what I thought, but a 'thank you' still seemed the right thing."

He tilted his head to one side, and his voice softened. "Did your Ma teach you those manners?"

"She did." I smiled, remembering how when I'd run away four years ago, everyone I met said I had good manners and my ma must have taught them to me. "She was a good mother and didn't deserve to die trying to have sons for a man who saw her as nothing but someone to breed." I was shaking inside, the memories stirring wounds that were always just below the surface.

He gave me a sideways look, his forehead furrowing, and I guessed he saw how my mood had darkened.

"I'm sorry," he said. "I didn't know."

"And you didn't bother to find out, either."

He didn't say anything to that, just sort of let it hang there for a while. Then he cleared his throat. "Like I said, I was young and stupid, but I should have found out. I didn't have to do anything if you were okay. But I should have found out."

"You got that right."

He let out a heavy breath. "I understand why you're mad at me. I've been angry at my mother ever since she left me in Illinois and went off to California with her new husband and my sisters and brother."

"Your mother left you? Why?"

"My father died when I was seven. I had two sisters and a brother younger than me. My mother couldn't make enough money taking in laundry and sewing to feed all of us, so she found a farmer willing to take me in as a bound boy. He agreed to provide food and clothes, send me to school, and teach me farming. I learned farming, but I never got to go to school. That's why I didn't write to your mother. I didn't know how."

Miz Wilma always said that everyone has a story, and Quinn's was beginning to sound interesting. "So how long did you have to work for the farmer?"

"The indenture was until I was eighteen, but I ran away when I was sixteen. I thought I could get rich as a fur trapper and trader, but by the time I got in, the price of beaver pelts had dropped. The big money was over. Sort of the story of my life." He pulled his mule to a stop. "This looks like a good place to eat. Hungry?"

"Yes."

We stopped where there was a large flat rock to sit on and an aspen grove with green leaves shimmering in the breeze. He opened a deerskin bag and removed pieces of hardtack and pemmican. I added peppermints for dessert.

After we finished eating, he took up his story again.

"I was with the farmer for about a year when my mother married and went to California with her new husband and my sisters and brother. She came to tell me they were going, and she was sorry I couldn't go because of the indenture contract with the farmer, and that's the last I heard from her. Well, she might have written, but I never got a letter, and I couldn't have read it anyway, but I could have got somebody to read it for me."

"Just like you could have gotten someone to write to my ma for you," I said.

He nodded. "Now you say it, I see I could've. But I didn't."

"So what happened next?"

"I worked and learned farming, that's for sure. I kept thinking if Ma's new husband did well, he might buy me out of the contract, but that didn't happen. Then, like I said, I heard all the stories about men getting rich trapping beaver and off I went.

"After I was foolish enough to leave Minerva, I stayed here in the mountains for a while, trapping, making enough to get by. Then in '49, gold was found in California, so I headed west. While I was there, I asked around about the man my mother married. I found out he owned a store and a saloon. My brother was set up in a freighting business. My sisters had married professional men, two lawyers."

"So did you talk to them?"

"No. I figured they got along fine without me. I'd just be a bother." He smiled and looked at me. "Unlike you, I didn't have the guts to walk up and ask my mother 'Why did you leave me? Was there something wrong with me that you kept your other kids and left me behind?' Takes more courage than what I had. I didn't want to hear her say I didn't matter."

Not mattering was what I had feared most about meeting him. It was a good thing I had finished eating because I got a huge lump in my throat, finding out he'd had the same feeling about his mother.

He stood and dusted himself off. "We'd best get going. It's a long way down the canyon. I'd like to find a place to camp for the night that provides an easy lookout. Not sure Sims can keep his kid reined in after dark."

"I spent the night with Max on the way up. We could stop there."

He stopped cold and stared at me. "Who's Max and what were you doing spending the night with him?"

"Well, don't you just sound like someone's father?" My lips twitched as I fought back a smile. "Thought you weren't interested in family."

"Don't try to sidetrack the subject. Who's Max?"

"A fellow I met when I was a boy. Which reminds me; I'd better put my hair up and my cap on. Max's mining partner thinks I am a boy."

"Who's Max?" he asked again.

"You're sounding like a parrot, repeating everything I say." I was enjoying this sudden show of fatherly concern and wanted to draw it out as long as possible, but by the tone of his voice, I'd probably gone as far as I could. It was time to tell a story of my own.

"When I was thirteen, I ran away, heading for Westport and Aunt Hannah. Ma was with child again and sick in bed most of the time. And Hiram was giving me looks."

"What kind of looks?"

I rolled my eyes. "You know what kind. The kind a man gives a girl with bosoms who's not his daughter."

The way Quinn's face was turning red and his eyes blazing, I figured I'd better try to calm him down. "He never did anything. I ran off when I saw his look. Anyway, back to Max. The first town I came to was Pawnee. I found work cleaning a stable in exchange for a place to sleep and a meal. I got woke up by shouts, and it was Max arguing with some gambler about Max's sister. Max claimed the man was ruining her. They argued, and Max shot him dead. Then he ran into the stable to get a horse and make a getaway. He saw me and took me hostage, making me get on the horse. He got on behind me. We rode off, and while we were running from the law, he put his hands on my chest and right away figured out I was a girl. He made this big gasp and moved his hands real fast.

"Once we outran the posse, he let me go. But later, he kept showing up in places I stopped. He said he'd delayed my trip and wanted to make sure I got where I was going okay." I slipped a sideways glance at Quinn. His face was back to a normal color. "Aunt Hannah said Max must like me, or he wouldn't have spent all that time making sure I got to Westport safe and sound."

His eyes narrowed, and he gave me a full-on look. "You trying to get a rise out of me?"

I was caught, and now that I thought about it, what I had done was dumb. "I was, and that was stupid. I just realized you're sort of the law around here, and Max is still a wanted man. He's really a good person. He never laid an improper hand on me once he knew I was a girl."

"The only place I have any claim to the law is Sims Gulch. Truth is, I might be wanted somewhere myself for all the foolish things I did when I was young."

I sighed. "Thank you."

***

We picked our way down the mountain without incident until we came to the next mining settlement, the one where Max worked a claim with Howie. There was still an hour of daylight left, but Quinn thought it best we camp in the company of others, thinking Bob Sims might come after us. Finding us among many would be more difficult than if we were alone.

I guided him to Max's camp. No one was there, so we took a seat on a couple of boulders. I scanned the tents and piles of dirt scattered across the mountainside with barely a foot of undisturbed land anywhere.

Quinn was evaluating the place, too. "Wonder how long this vein will last? You get this many men working, most of the easy gold gives out before long."

"I guess that means you won't be around here much longer," I said.

"Probably a month or less."

We heard the crunch of footsteps on the rocks.

"Cord, you're back," Max said.

"Hi, Max. This is my uncle, Justin Quinn."

The two men shook hands.

"I guess you're the family Cord was looking for," Max said.

"Yes," Quinn said. "I'm seeing him back to Denver. He had a run-in with one of the Sims boys up the canyon. Cord says you're a friend and might let us bed down here tonight."

"Sure thing."

Max was carrying a thin rope with three fish strung on it. "Trout," he said, raising them chest high. "I caught us some supper." He looked at me, his mouth twitching. "Guess it's your turn to do the cleaning." He picked up a pan and held it and the fish out to me.

I laughed, remembering our previous fishing experience and the fish that landed in his lap.

Quinn took over then. "Since you're sharing the catch, it's only right I do the cleaning." He took the pan and string of fish and headed for the creek, leaving Max and me alone.

Max sat on a flat stone next to mine, folded his arms, and asked, "So who is this Quinn really?"

"He's my father. Remember Mr. O'Rourke, the 'Lothario' you warned me about? Turns out Mr. O'Rourke is a friend of Aunt Hannah's. He heard from Miz Wilma that she knew my father's whereabouts, so I came out to see if I could find him."

"So that family member story you told was true but not complete?"

"Yes."

"So why the story about him being your uncle?"

"Because my last name is Pierce and people think I'm a boy. Or they did until Bob Sims knocked off my hat and my hair came down. Then he knew I was the girl he had traveled on the stagecoach with from Junction City to Denver. He is an ill-mannered boor. We didn't get along on the stage, and he was glad to have a chance to cause me trouble. Fast thinking made Quinn my uncle."

"You have a lot of trouble with that passing-as-a-boy thing. Maybe you should give it up."

"If men weren't such goats, maybe I might."

"Ouch!"

"You deserve it."

We sat for a minute, and then I asked, "What about Marlon and Macawi? Did you come back to the mountains with them?"

"Yes, we spent a winter trapping. Then I headed for California, arriving too late for any easy gold there, so I returned to the Rockies and trapping, working my way down from the north. I met Howie in California. When we heard about gold here, we decided to try prospecting again." He sighed. "This canyon's getting crowded."

Howie ambled up and set his pan beside Max on the rock. "Sure is. Every day, there's more sand in the pan and less color." He jerked his head toward the creek. "Fellow down at the creek cleaning fish says his name's Quinn and he's passing through with this one." He squinted at me.

"Hello, Howie," I said. "Yes, that's my uncle. He's going down to Denver where I'm catching the stage back to Westport and he's picking up supplies. He has a claim up in Sims Gulch."

Howie looked relieved, like he thought I or Quinn might be trying to muscle in on his territory. He tossed his poke beside the pan on the rock. "Probably five dollars in dust there. How'd you do?"

"About the same." Max reached for his poke and tossed it beside the other one. "That's still good compared to working below ground for someone else, but we need to be thinking of where to go next."

Howie looked at me. "Suppose we talk about that tomorrow when our company's gone?"

Max nodded. "Sure."

Quinn trudged up the mountain carrying a pan full of cleaned fish. "Here's the food. Who's the cook?"

I shook my head. "It had better be someone with more experience cooking over campfires than I have."

Max laughed. "I caught them. I'll cook them."

He rustled around in his tent and came back with some cornmeal to coat the fish, some lard, and an iron skillet. Within minutes, the fish were sizzling in the pan. The smell of frying food churned up hunger pangs in my stomach.

We ate, and then the men talked of where they'd been and adventures they'd had. Max and Howie had been to many of the places Quinn and Coop had been, just different times. Howie seemed to relax as he got to know Quinn better and realized he wasn't trying to move in on Howie's territory.

All was calm by the time we turned in for the night.

***

We left Max's claim at first light and reached Denver that evening without incident. Miz Wilma greeted us. "That didn't take long. Are you going to introduce me?"

"As if you didn't already know," I said. "This is Justin Quinn, my father. And this is Miz Wilma, who you have heard so much about on the way here."

Quinn took Miz Wilma's hand and squeezed it. "Haven't we met before? Six weeks or so ago up near Sims Gulch? You were traveling with some trappers and helped set a broken arm."

"Yes, and not three hours later, I slipped on some rocks and had my own broken bone." She waved a hand at her bandaged limb.

Quinn smiled. "It's an honor to formally meet you. Thank you for looking out for Cordelia and helping her find her way to me."

Miz Wilma gave him that look she had when she was evaluating someone. Then with a nod, she said, "I'm right glad it worked out for both of you."

I glanced at Quinn. "It was touch and go at first. It was that mean-tempered Bob Sims that brought us together, so I guess there is something to thank him for."

"I couldn't let Cordelia travel alone knowing he might follow her," Quinn said. "It gave us more time to get to know each other."

"Like you always say, Miz Wilma, everyone has a story, and Quinn and I got a chance to trade ours."

"Quinn? That's what you're calling him?" She glanced at Quinn. "You all right with that?"

He nodded. "I'm getting used to it."

"Me, too," I said. It was like Mr. O'Rourke had told me; when you get used to calling someone a certain name, it's hard to change. Besides, as much as I'd come to understand what Quinn had done and why he hadn't come looking for me, he still didn't seem like a person I could call pa, even though I had introduced him to Miz Wilma as my father.

Miz Wilma said, "I'm about ready to leave here and head back east. I'll be stopping in to visit those two little ones I picked up at the Indian school at St. Marys. They're like godchildren to me now."

"When are you leaving, Miz Wilma?" I asked.

"Tomorrow, I reckon. I was just waiting for you to get back with the mules."

"Then I should come with you. You'll need help gathering firewood and hauling water, and we're going in the same direction. It'll save me stage fare."

Quinn frowned at me. "Will you be safe?"

Miz Wilma's eyes twinkled. "Spoken like a true father. She'll be safe. I have plenty of friends among the tribes." She glanced up as Bart and Selma entered.

"Hello, Cordelia," Bart said. "We saw the mules and knew you were back. Good thing. Miz Wilma, here, has been itching to get on the road."

Selma said, "Would you like coffee?"

"No, thank you," Quinn said. "I need to get a room and a shower." He glanced at me. "What about you? Are you coming with me?"

"Yes," I said. "I'd like to get cleaned up before I get back on the trail. But don't expect more than a basin of water for washing. That's all the one hotel I found provided."

Bart spoke up. "There's a bath house on down the block from the hotel. I wouldn't recommend it for a young lady alone, but since your father's with you. . ."

"What do you think, Cordelia?" Quinn asked. "Want to give it a try?"

I rubbed my hand across the back of my head, feeling the oily heaviness of hair unwashed for over two weeks. "I do," I said. "Miz Wilma, I'll go unload Waiting and put everything in my trunk. Thanks for the loan of the saddlebags. I'll be back tomorrow at first light."

"I'll help you," Quinn said. "Thanks, again." He shook hands all around.

Outside, we took the bags off Waiting and tied the mules where they could drink and eat. I kept one bag that had my bloomers, a dress, and clean underwear. Then Quinn led his mule while we walked to the hotel. After Quinn checked us in, we went to our rooms to leave our belongings, then walked the half-block to the bath house. Quinn carried two wool blankets to use for drying off. Four men stood in line ahead of us, but showers went quick.

When our turn came, Quinn handed me a bar of soap, and I went in first. There were two small rooms, one for removing clothes and one for showering. I took off my boy clothes down to my shirt and underwear. It seemed strange to leave clothes on while bathing, but I couldn't take everything off in such a public place even though no one could see me. After letting my hair down, I stepped into a small room with metal sides and floor. There were holes in the flooring to drain the water. I pulled a chain and cold water poured down on me.

Shivering, I used my handkerchief to soap my hair, face, and body before pulling the chain again for a rinse. Being drenched twice with cold water was all I could take. I wrapped myself in the wool blanket and rubbed my hair and skin, drying off as best I could before donning my pants and jacket and twisting my hair in a bun. I put on my cap and pulled the damp blanket high around my face and shoulders to keep anyone from guessing I was a woman.

After my shower, Quinn took his while I rushed to my room to comb my hair and change into my girl clothes. I donned a chemise that came to my knees and my usual three ankle-length petticoats, Then I slipped into a green calico skirt and matching bodice.

Quinn knocked at my door when he was ready to take me to supper. His eyes lit up when he saw me. "You look like your mother, you know."

The compliment made me proud. I touched the pendant containing her hair and smiled.

We went to the dining room that seemed more like a saloon than a place to eat. He bought me a meal of fried chicken, potatoes and gravy, and biscuits, along with a big slice of apple pie for dessert. The place might look like a combination saloon and gambling hall, but they had good cooks.

When we'd finished our pie and were lingering over coffee, I asked, "So you'll be leaving Sims Gulch soon to go looking for gold somewhere else?"

He nodded. "Will you be going to stay with your aunt?"

"Yes."

"So if I send you a letter there, you'll get it?"

"A letter?"

"Coop taught me to write. We could keep in touch."

"I'd like that," I said. "I'll write back."

We left it at that. Quinn paid the bill, and we went upstairs.

At the door to my room, Quinn said, "Let's meet in the morning before you leave. Knock on my door if I'm not up yet."

"I will. Good night."

***

I had a hard time going to sleep. In spite of what Miz Wilma had said about our journey east being safe, the land itself worried me more than Indians or robbers. I had seen how dry a large part of the countryside was, how absent of animals and water. Further east were the giant herds of buffalo that might stampede and trample us. Even though Miz Wilma had made the trip many times, she hadn't done it with a weakened leg. I was certain her bone hadn't completely healed, but I knew how much she loved to travel. She had helped me when I most needed it. I had to do the same for her.

Unable to sleep, I lit a lantern, removed a sheet of stationery from my handbag, and began a letter to Aunt Hannah to tell her it would be two months before I arrived in Westport. I tried to keep misgivings out of the message, but I wasn't completely successful. By the time I addressed and sealed my letter, I was sure she would worry when she read it. But she would worry more if she heard nothing from me, so I had done the best I could.

With the task completed, I returned to bed and slept at least two hours before being awakened by the call of nature. After using the chamber pot, I put on the dress I'd worn the night before, thinking that once on the trail away from Denver, I would change to boy's clothes or bloomers, whichever seemed best. I would get Miz Wilma's advice on the matter. It seemed ridiculous in the middle of a wild, unsettled land to be worried about fashion approval. But there it was. There was always someone wanting to put women in their place. Luckily for Miz Wilma, she seemed to be past that need for approval. Wherever she went, people accepted her as a healer, a bit eccentric but worth allowances. Would there ever be a day when the same would be true for me?

There was a knock at the door. "Cordelia? Are you awake?" It was Quinn.

"Coming." I laid my comb aside and opened the door.

"Ah, up and dressed," he said.

"Yes, I'm gathering my belongings now." I picked up the letter and slipped it in my handbag. "I need to leave this at the desk for mailing."

Quinn looked around the room and picked up the satchel containing my clothes. "Is there anything else?"

"No." We started down the stairs. "Are you staying over another day to buy supplies?"

"It won't take long to buy what I need. I'll be on my way up the mountain by midmorning." His eyes narrowed. "You're sure about what you're doing. It's a dangerous trip, more so with just you and that old woman."

I bristled at the hint I should change my plans. "That old woman has done so much for me that I can't let her go alone. I have to do what is right, no matter the danger."

He sighed. "I was afraid you were going to say that. It will take you weeks to get home. By then, my letter will be waiting for you. Let me know when you arrive."

I smiled at his concern. "I will."

We loaded my belongings onto his mule and strolled down the almost vacant street as the sun's first rays beamed on the horizon, lighting the clouds in shades of pink. The air was fresh and cool, the breeze light. A perfect day for travel.

When we arrived at Bart and Selma's tent, Miz Wilma was leaning on a cane, hobbling around, hitching up Ready and Waiting for the trip. Duke wagged his tail. Quinn hefted my bag to the wagon seat. "Let me help with that," he said, taking the reins and putting Ready in place.

"Can you make it onto the wagon?" I asked Miz Wilma.

"Bart made me steps." She jerked her head to one side.

I looked in that direction and saw a set of wooden steps, four up.

Quinn finished hitching the mules and went to pick up the steps and put them in place for her.

"Thank you, Mr. Quinn," she said. "Looks like Cordelia did all right after all when it comes to fathers."

Quinn ducked his head at the compliment. "Thank you."

"You're right, Miz Wilma. I ended up getting the best of what I imagined instead of the worst."

"And you, Mr. Quinn. What do you think of Cordelia?"

"I think I'm a lucky man and proud to be her father or her uncle or whoever else she needs me to be at any given time."

"I like that answer." I glanced at Miz Wilma who already had the reins in her hand. "It's time to go."

He took my hands. "I'm glad you came. Remember to write when you get home."

I bit my lip. "I will."

He let go my hands and circled me for a moment with his arms. "Take care." Then he stood back, gave a long look, and let go.

After I climbed on the wagon, he loaded the steps in the back.

Miz Wilma shook the reins, shouted "Giddap," and we were on our way.

15) MATCHMAKING

Lucy

I decided to follow Ambrose's suggestion about pleasing Pa. It took a few days, but he did start to lighten up. Mrs. Collins helped by inviting us to dinner after church the next Sunday. I replied I was looking forward to it, but she had to come and sample my cooking because the invitations couldn't all be one-sided. Pa was pleased about the invitation, which made me wonder if he'd truly given up on marrying Mrs. Collins. Except for being too old to have babies, she seemed like a good match for him. If I could get something going between them, he might be too busy courting her to look for a beau for me. If Mrs. Collins didn't work out, maybe some other woman would. Of course, finding another woman would be a challenge. Single ones of marrying age were snapped up fast in Hidden Springs.

I invited Mrs. Collins for Wednesday evening. This being my first complete meal to fix for company, I wanted it to be perfect. I figured I'd use some garden produce. Pa wasn't into what he called rabbit food, but I was betting Mrs. Collins was because she served some in the dining hall of her boardinghouse. I picked greens, planning to heat them and season with oil and vinegar. I fretted over what meat to serve until Ambrose came in that morning with fresh catfish from the river. Fish with some rice and biscuits would make a fine meal. I'd top it off with slices of my prize-winning peach pie for dessert.

After I got the food worked out, I settled down with some of the furniture wish-books. Ambrose had told me to pick out a dining table and chairs, and he would make a set like it. We had Ma's walnut buffet, which was still a fine piece of furniture now that the mirror had been replaced, the drawers repaired, and the wood refinished, but it stood all alone in the dining room. Serving guests in the kitchen was beneath Pa's ambitions to be seen as a successful, important member of the town, so I needed to do something quick. Also, there was the matter of wall covering such as paper or cloth. And what about pictures, either photographs or paintings? I was getting a headache thinking of it all.

After flipping through the furniture wish-books, I picked out a walnut table and chairs. They looked solid and impressive. There was a big chair with arms for the head of the table. I knew Pa would like that. The set included a special chair for the woman of the house. I wondered if I would fill that seat until I could find Pa a wife.

With that decided, I looked through Ma's cookbook for a catfish recipe. I'd never cooked fish, but how hard could it be?

***

Pa went to fetch Mrs. Collins while I was putting the finishing touches on supper. The fish was frying and the rice simmering. The biscuits had risen well, and the tops were golden brown. I took the pan from the oven and moved the biscuits to a basket with a hot stone in the bottom. I heard Pa come in with Mrs. Collins, their voices drifting from the front hallway, so I draped a towel over the biscuits to keep them warm, wiped my hands on my apron, and went to the kitchen door to greet them. We had just finished our hellos when I smelled something burning.

"The rice! Oh no." I ran for the stove, pulled the pan from the fire, and stared into the pot. The rice had boiled dry and started to burn around the sides. Why couldn't I ever get this right?

Mrs. Collins came up behind me. "This kind of thing happens to everyone, Lucy. We still have the fish, which looks a nice golden brown and ready to remove from the skillet. And do I smell biscuits?"

I nodded and pointed at the basket.

She raised the towel. "Perfect. They have risen well. Now, you serve up the rest of the meal, and I'll take these biscuits to the table."

"Thank you," I said.

Pa scowled. "Fine how-do-you-do when the guest has to put the meal on the table."

Mrs. Collins tried to calm him. "I don't mind, Hiram. Putting a meal together for company isn't as easy as it looks."

"Humph."

I clamped my mouth shut, and my throat got sore from pushing back my hurt feelings.

Ambrose came in and took a seat at the table.

Pa kept up his grumbling, apologizing to Mrs. Collins. "Sorry about eating in the kitchen. Lucy is supposed to do something about decorating the dining room, but she hasn't gotten around to doing anything about that yet."

"I picked out a table and chairs this afternoon," I said as I set the platter of fish in front of Pa and went back to the counter for the bowl of greens and the butter.

Once we were all seated, Pa said grace, something he always did when there was company, and we passed the food around.

Pa was first to bite into the fish. "Overdone," he said, plunking his fork on his plate. "You ruined half the meal. Nothing fit to eat but rabbit food and biscuits. I sure don't want the rabbit food. A fine meal for company."

Wanting to die of embarrassment and shame, I scooted my chair back. "Excuse me," I said, but I didn't wait to be excused before fleeing the kitchen. I raced up the stairs and into my room, flung myself onto the bed, and let go of the sobs that had been choking me. I was a failure.

There was a knock at the door.

"Lucy," Mrs. Collins said. "May I come in?"

I pushed up on my elbows. "Yes."

She crossed to the bed and handed me a handkerchief.

I dried my tears, sniffling, trying to get control of myself. "I'm sorry about ruining the meal. Everything was going fine, and then I forgot to keep watch, and overcooked everything. Pa's so mad at me."

She sat on the edge of the bed and patted my back. "I've already told your pa that his behavior in front of a guest was unacceptable. Lucy, you did the best you could. There's no point in someone making it worse with a tantrum, and I told him that."

"I guess you wouldn't consider marrying Pa now."

Mrs. Collins clapped a hand over her mouth and her shoulders shook as she let go with a belly laugh. When at last she calmed down, she said, "Not now or ever. What put that idea in your head?"

"When Ma was sick and Pa laid up with the burn and broken ribs, Ma said you and the rest of us looked like a perfect family without her because you got along so well with Pa."

Mrs. Collins tilted her head sideways, pressed her lips together, and nodded. "I do remember Minerva saying that I got along better with Hiram than any other woman she knew, but I told her the truth about that. I got along with him because I wasn't married to him." She patted my shoulder. "Hiram asked me to marry him not long after your mother passed. I turned him down. He's my friend, but sometimes he behaves horribly, like he did tonight. If we were married, I'd have to say something, like I did tonight. But he wouldn't put up with what I said if we were married. He'd be putting me in my place, which as a wife would be to obey him and never question or criticize his words or actions."

I flipped over and sat up. "I figured if he was busy courting someone and getting married, he wouldn't have so much time to find a husband for me." I pulled my knees to my chest and wrapped my arms around them. "Can you think of anyone else he might marry?"

Her eyes sparkled. "You're a determined matchmaker. To be honest, after his proposal, I tried to think of someone for him. He was all alone here with Ambrose, and they both needed a woman's touch, but I couldn't find anyone who seemed right. There was the schoolteacher last fall, but come spring, she married a soldier."

I perked up at the mention of schoolteachers. "Pa introduced me to a man teacher from Ft. Riley, like he might be suitable for me. So if we find a new woman teacher for Hidden Springs, maybe she will like Pa and marry him. Who will hire the new teacher? The mayor? Do you have a say?"

"As a businesswoman, I have some influence with the men who do the hiring. And I will keep your request in mind—a suitable match for Hiram. Who knows, she might continue teaching after marriage if someone could get the board to change the 'single teacher' rule, and we could stop having to find a replacement every school year. But you do know, Lucy, that your pa will still be determined to find a suitable match for you."

"But I'm not ready to get married and have babies every year and maybe die like Ma. And I don't want to marry someone ten or fifteen years older than I am."

"Unfortunately, those are the men who are established in the world, the men who can give you a good life filled with comforts. That's what your father wants for you, a young man of twenty-five or older who is established in a business or profession. A doctor, a teacher, a lawyer, a minister, all fine professional men. Younger than that, they're all boys trying to figure out what to do with their lives."

"Then why can't I wait to get married until I'm twenty-five?"

"Back east, all the good men would be taken by then, and you'd be an old maid forever. But it might be possible out here where men outnumber women."

"You're saying the same things Aunt Hannah and Cordelia say with their suffragette and equal rights for women speeches. Are you one of them?"

Mrs. Collins smiled. "No, at least, not openly, but I do believe a woman has the right to speak her mind and have her words considered. She should also have a right to say no to a marriage if the man is someone she cannot see spending her life with. To that end, I shall try to stall your father's search for a husband he considers suitable and help you in your quest for one you will enjoy having as a life partner."

I hugged her. "Thank you for understanding."

She pushed me back, gripped my shoulders, and looked me in the eye. "Don't misunderstand me. I'll do my best, but I can't guarantee your father will listen."

"Just knowing I'm not all alone in this helps. I have so longed for someone to talk to. Susan Hogan helped me make a winning peach pie, and Pa won't even let me visit with her."

"That's too bad. Everyone needs friends. Are you ready to come downstairs and make up with your father?"

"I guess. Although, it isn't always possible. He just stays mad."

"I told you we had a talk. He'll be nice, at least until after he takes me home."

I scooted off the bed, smoothed my skirt, and stood tall. "All right, let's go."

***

The day after my failed meal, I told Pa I wanted to join the choir and asked his permission to attend practice that afternoon. I had sung in the choir at Aunt Hilda's church, so I figured that was a good place to meet possible marriage prospects for Pa. He said I could go, but I had to stop by the smithy on my way home to let him know how it went.

I supposed he wanted to make sure I didn't spend any time with the Hogans, but I didn't care as long as I could go.

It felt good to walk alone in the afternoon sun. I kept my head turned away from the Hogan's cabin as I was passing, but slanted my eyes sideways from time to time, hoping to catch a glance of Willy and then hoping not to since if Pa heard I'd been talking to him, I'd probably be locked in our house for life.

Most of the choir was present when I entered the church. An old upright piano occupied the left side of the stage, which was one step up from the main floor. Two benches for the choir were in the center with a pulpit for the preacher to the right. Reverend Sherwood was in shirtsleeves at a desk in a tiny office off the sanctuary. I was the tenth member of the singing group. Besides the preacher, three men and six women plus the pianist were present.

After a round of introductions, I saw only one possibility for Pa. Ava Carstairs was new in town, too. She'd arrived four weeks ago—a few days before me—to stay with the Fletchers who owned the general store. Their unmarried cousin, she appeared to about thirty years old. More stylish than pretty, she was about my height, large-boned, and solidly built, like she could have babies and whip up a meal or scrub clothes at the same time. She had parted her dark auburn hair down the middle and twisted it into a tight bun. She wore a high-necked, rust-colored calico dress with tiny, white flowers in the design. The way the skirt stood out, I figured she had to be wearing one of the new cage crinoline hoop skirts like Aunt May had. Pa would probably like that since he prided himself on having all the latest and best.

After I sang a few bars, Reverend Sherwood determined I was an alto and put me beside Miss Carstairs, who was also an alto. We shared a tattered hymnbook. I hoped we had raised enough money at the pie sale to get new books. What we had were castoffs from a church back east.

The pianist played "Rock of Ages" while Reverend Sherwood conducted. In all, we practiced three hymns.

When choir practice ended, we all stood. I put the hymnbook on the table near the piano and hurried to catch up with Miss Carstairs who was halfway to the front of the church.

"You have a lovely voice," I said, hoping the compliment would lead to a conversation.

"Thank you," she said, continuing on her way, not even pausing to look at me.

Clearly, she considered me a pesky child not worth her attention. I searched for something to say that might interest her, but I didn't know what we might have in common besides the practice.

Then I thought of the general store.

"Your dress is made of such pretty material. Do you have any like it at the store?"

She slowed, and glanced at me, raising an eyebrow. "Not exactly like it. But there are similar patterns in this color. Do you sew?"

"Oh, yes," I said. "My mother taught me before she passed away." I paused. "Now my pa, Hiram Pierce, the blacksmith, has a new house that needs lots of decorating. You know, wall coverings and draperies. I imagine I'll be spending a lot of time selecting all those items."

She looked at me full on now, paying me some attention since there might be money to be made. "A new house, you say?"

"A two-story stone house north of town about a mile. It's the last one on Pierce Road. My pa is on the town council, you know, and ours was one of the first families to move here."

She perked up at that. "I didn't know. Perhaps you'd like to walk along to the store with me. We have a wall covering sample book you might find helpful."

"That would be wonderful. Before I decide, though, maybe you could visit sometime to see the rooms. I think some patterns are better for large rooms than others. You could help me choose if you saw the space."

By this time, we were almost in front of the smithy, so I asked, "Have you met my pa?"

"I don't believe so."

"Let's say hello. He wanted me to stop by and tell him how the choir practice went."

"W-e-l-l-l," she said, drawing out the word, reluctant.

"He'll be glad to meet you and know someone is going to help me with the decorating. He'll be relieved. I've been staying with my aunt in Westport since Ma passed away. Before I came, I sort of led him to believe I knew more about making a home than I do. I'm afraid I've been a disappointment so far. Last night, I even burned the rice."

"I suppose if it will ease his mind. . . ."

"He's worried I'll buy the wrong thing and turn the dining room and parlor into a disaster."

"Well, then," she said, "let's put his mind at ease."

We entered the smithy to the sound of hammer on iron. Pa wore a heavy leather apron to protect his chest from sparks from the fire. His sleeves were rolled up. His arm muscles tightened as he raised the hammer and brought it down on the iron. I could see Miss Carstairs was impressed.

"Pa," I called out.

He laid the hammer aside. "What?" His voice was gruff. Then he looked up and saw I was not alone.

"Hello," he said, his tone friendly. He reached for a rag and wiped his hands. "Can I help you?"

"Actually, Pa," I said, "she has offered to help us. This is Miss Ava Carstairs. She is a cousin of the Fletchers and is working in their store. She's had a lot of experience in decorating, and she offered to advise me on the wall and window coverings."

Pa came towards us out of the dimness of the shop to the door where natural light gave him a better view of Miss Carstairs.

"It's nice to meet you, Miss Carstairs. I believe I did see you at the pie contest and sale, but I was busy entertaining a guest."

"It's nice to meet you as well, Mr. Pierce. Your daughter speaks highly of you, and her dearest wish is that she will please you with a beautifully appointed home."

Pa was all smiles at that.

Miss Carstairs continued. "Your daughter is an intelligent young lady but inexperienced. However, by the time we have your home decorated, she should be able to furnish her own home tastefully someday."

"That is exactly what I want for her," Pa said, his face beaming.

It was working. I had found the perfect woman for Pa. I was sure of it.

***

After meeting Pa, Miss Carstairs was eager to get started on decorating our house. We stopped by the general store to pick up a wallpaper sample book. Her cousin hitched a horse to the buckboard for us. Miss Carstairs didn't favor carrying such a large book a mile to my house and back to the store in her arms.

When we turned off the main road onto the circle drive, she pulled the horse to a stop. "Well," she said, "that is a fine home."

"Pa and my brother built it. It was mostly Ambrose that cut the stone. He apprenticed to a stone mason for two years so he could learn how."

"How old is your brother?"

I saw right away where she was going with that question. "A year older than me. Fourteen."

"Oh."

I figured that meant she realized he was too young for her and my pa was the best match after all.

We went on up the drive. She set the brake, and we tied the reins to the post.

She eyed the grounds. "There should be flowers in front and a bush or two. The outside of a house is as important as the interior."

I sighed. "So much to think about. I'm overwhelmed."

She patted my shoulder. "Don't fret. We will do one thing at a time, and someday it will be finished."

"Thank you so much for offering to help," I said. One thing at a time. That sounded like the decorating would take long enough to get Pa and her together.

I showed her the dining room first. The buffet was in there, so the room wasn't completely empty.

"That's a lovely piece of furniture," she said.

"It's the only thing we brought with us from Westport."

"What about the dining table and chairs?"

"We sold them and most of the other pieces. There wasn't room in the wagon for everything." I pointed at the furniture catalog on the top of the buffet. "I'm looking at styles. Ambrose is going to build whatever I like."

"A stone mason and a carpenter. Ambrose sounds very talented."

"He does some blacksmithing, too. He worked in the shop with Pa until he apprenticed with the stone mason."

"Ambrose sounds like a fine catch for some young lady."

"Years from now, I guess he will be. Mrs. Collins says hardly any man is worth marrying until he's at least twenty-five or so. Did I mention Ambrose is only fourteen?"

She laughed. "Yes, you did."

She placed the wallcovering book on the buffet beside the furniture catalog, and we browsed through page after page of floral design patterns in different shapes and colors. Then I turned the last page, and my eyebrows shot up at some kind of Greek design with an almost naked man standing in front of a rearing horse. There was a second horse and a boy with only a robe over his shoulder, which, thankfully, covered his private parts. My mouth fell open.

Miss Carstairs ducked her head and pressed her lips together, stifling a laugh. "I suppose your father would not want that design on his walls."

I flipped back to a floral design. "He'd be mad that I even saw it."

"So what do you like?" she asked.

I picked a range of three each of the large, medium, and small floral patterns in different colors, figuring she could tell me which she liked. That worked.

She chose three floral motifs of green, blue, and gray with contrasting backgrounds. "Now that we have them narrowed down, let's get your father's opinion. After all, it is his house."

"Of course," I said. "What about the parlor? Should we use the same covering there or something different?"

"Something different. Let's have a look at it. We'll leave the sample book here."

I led the way to the parlor, empty except for Ma's rocking chair and the fireplace that occupied a large part of one wall. Miss Carstairs ran her hand along the dark walnut wood of the mantle.

Light streamed in the tall windows. She crossed the room and peered out one of them. "Oh, there's a cabin in back."

"Pa built it when we first settled here. I think he's saving it for Ambrose when he gets married someday."

"If Mrs. Collins is right about a man not marrying until he is at least twenty-five, then that cabin will be empty a long time."

"Yes." I shivered. Talking about the cabin reminded me of Ma dying there.

"What's wrong, Lucy?"

"Nothing. Where are my manners? I haven't even offered you tea. And I have sugar cookies. I'm sorry to have to serve them in the kitchen."

"I'd love to have a cup of tea."

When we walked into the kitchen, I tried to see it as I thought she would. The table was square oak, and the chairs were oak as well. Ambrose had made them, sanded and finished them with shellac.

"A separate room for cooking. Your father is progressive in his thinking." Miss Carstairs ran her hand along the smooth top of the worktable. "Nicely done. I suppose this is another sample of Ambrose's work."

"Yes, ma'am."

"And the iron cook stove?"

"Pa made that." There was room on top for three pots or skillets. The oven would hold a turkey. "I baked three loaves of bread in it at once. And there's room for a big pan of cookies or biscuits." I tried to think of all the pluses the kitchen had that might make a woman want it for her own.

There were only two small windows on the back wall, one on either side of the door. A view out those windows would show the cabin again, and I didn't want to see it. "We don't have curtains yet," I said, "so I need to make those, and a rag rug for the floor."

She nodded as she opened the door to the pie safe.

"I'll put water on for tea," I said. Crossing to the stove, I started a fire in the firebox and then dipped water from a bucket into the teapot. Opening the pie safe, I pulled out a plate of cookies and set it on the table.

Miss Carstairs settled at the table, looked out the window, and frowned.

I followed her gaze and saw she was looking at our old cabin.

***

I had supper ready when Pa and Ambrose came home, and I didn't burn or overcook anything. Ambrose said as much. Pa was silent on the subject.

Since Pa didn't seem in a talking mood, I decided I would have to steer the conversation to house decorating.

"Miss Carstairs was real impressed with the house," I said.

"Who is Miss Carstairs," Ambrose asked.

"Someone who thinks it's too bad you're not old enough to marry," I teased.

Pa straightened up when I said that. "What?"

"Well, she's a single lady, and she saw how good Ambrose was at building a house and making furniture, so, of course, she was interested in how old he was."

Ambrose's face flushed red.

"But I told her my pa made the cook stove, and she thought that was pretty nice work, too."

"Where'd you meet this Miss Carstairs and why was she in our house?" Ambrose asked.

Really, sometimes Ambrose sounded just like Pa. "At choir practice," I said. "She's cousin to the Fletchers and works at the general store. She's helping me pick out wall coverings and draperies. The sample book is in the dining room. I'll show you some of the patterns we picked out for Pa's approval." I jumped up from the table and hurried out of the room to give them time to think about what I'd said about Miss Carstairs. She was looking for a husband. I wondered if Pa would be flattered.

16) CROSSING THE PLAINS

Cordelia

We had been on the road three days, constantly meeting strings of go-backers who had come west without enough money and supplies to finance their prospecting and an equal number of folks heading to the mountains. The one group was depressed; the other excited. The go-backers moved at an even faster pace than the comers, running away from a bad experience, often leaving their possessions along the trail.

We traveled at a slow pace. Every time the wagon bounced, Miz Wilma winced with pain. But she had to ride, her leg not being well enough for walking such a great distance as we had in front of us.

After a full day on the trail, we paid a fee to stay the night and fill our barrels with water at one of the stage stations. We stopped at Station 24 along Big Sandy Creek, let the mules eat and drink their fill, and made camp for the night.

After a meal of beans and ship biscuit, we settled down beside the dying fire and drank our coffee, talking of the past, the country we had just crossed, and what we might encounter the following day.

"This route has changed since I came through last fall," Miz Wilma said. "Course, that whole stream of folks heading west practically ran me down in their rush to Pikes Peak. Now those folks are almost running over us going home. And a new crop coming. All these fools are going to ruin the mountains."

I nodded and petted Duke's head. He stiffened and stood up,

growling at a rider coming in from the west. Another go-backer, I supposed. "It's okay, Duke. Settle down."

But Duke didn't settle down. Instead, he kept up the low growl while the rider came to our campsite and dismounted.

Duke barked.

"Hush now," Miz Wilma said. "You'll wake up those that's sleeping."

Duke gave a whine of protest and settled down beside me.

"Thanks for calling off the dog, ma'am. Cordelia, tell him I'm a friend."

I squinted to see him, but I knew who he was by his voice.

"Max, what are you doing here?"

Miz Wilma leaned forward, her face lighting up. "This is Max? Come have a seat, boy. I've heard so much about you."

"Not everything, I hope."

"How was I to know you would show up?" I asked.

"Oh," he said, realizing Miz Wilma knew he was a wanted man.

"What are you doing here, Max?" I repeated, sounding like a pirate's parrot.

"Quinn stopped by on his way up the canyon. He told me you two ladies were out here alone, so I said I'd see you as far as Junction City."

"What about your claim?" I asked.

"Howie's going to sell it and join up with Quinn until I get back. Quinn said he was ready to move on to fresh diggings deeper into the mountains. He figures if he stays where he is, he'll have nothing but trouble from the Sims boys."

I made a face. "My fault."

"I doubt it. From what Quinn said, they're a bad lot and would have caused trouble even if you'd never come along."

Miz Wilma gave him one of her calculating looks. "Besides your name, who are you?"

"Cordelia's friend, I hope. I helped her hide her wanted poster and saw her all the way to Westport a few years back. When we traveled downriver with Marlon and Macawi, I caught the bigger fish."

I sputtered about how mine had been headless and tailless by the time he did the measuring, but then I saw Miz Wilma with her mouth open like she had something to say.

"Did you meet Marlon and Macawi's boy? I was there at his birthing."

"Sure did. But Cordelia had the most to do with him. Kept him from running off the side of the raft."

I laughed. "His first steps."

We continued trading stories until Miz Wilma was nodding. I touched her shoulder and roused her enough to help her into the wagon for a night's sleep. Then I tied the wagon flaps back so we could get a breeze.

Max bedded down by the dying ashes. Given the warmth of the night, he had the best spot.

I tried to sleep, but my mind had fastened on Aunt Hannah's words about Max liking me or he wouldn't have troubled himself seeing I made it safely all the way to Westport. Was that still true? And how did I feel about Max? Aunt Hannah seemed to think I liked him, too. Well, I did, but just as a friend. At least, I thought so.

***

The next morning I cooked oatmeal, and we flavored it with molasses, drank our coffee, and considered trail options.

"Smoky Hill would cut some miles," Miz Wilma said, "but there's no stage stations that way. Lots of folks have died crossing there."

"I'd rather take longer and not die of thirst," I said. "I bet Duke feels the same."

Miz Wilma raised an eyebrow at Max.

He shook his head. "I don't figure I have a say since I barged in, but following the stage route seems like our best chance of arriving safely."

"Well, then, since you young'uns are too soft for the Smoky Hill, we'll go northeast on the stage route."

We hitched up Ready and Waiting and headed out. As we traveled, Max shook his head every time we came to belongings the go-backers had tossed out. "If I were on my way to gold country, I'd be picking up that pan and pick," he said. "Seems like they would have sold it if they didn't want it. Supplies are hard to come by in the mine fields."

In fact, we passed folks going west who stopped to pick up some of the tossed items.

Miz Wilma was unhappy with what she saw. "Making the whole country a trash pile."

"Or a graveyard," I said, as we passed yet another mound of earth topped with a pile of stones. Some had makeshift crosses with names. Others were unmarked.

We traveled for a couple of hours without coming across anyone. Then a flash of red material fluttered in the wind. I squinted and saw a body in buckskin britches several yards from the trail. I reined the mules to a stop.

"Look, Max." I pointed toward the body.

Max's gaze followed my finger, and he rode over to investigate. Miz Wilma and I watched him dismount and squat beside the body.

"Hey, fella," he said and shook the shoulder.

A buckskinned leg twitched. Then a low moan.

Max opened his canteen, turned the fallen chap on his back, and held the canteen to his mouth.

I climbed out of the wagon and joined Max to get a better look. The boy was young, maybe Ambrose's age. What was he doing out here alone?

That wasn't hard to guess. Probably whoever he came with was in one of the graves we had passed.

He was sunburned and too weak to sit on his own. Max picked him up and carried him to the wagon.

Miz Wilma was alarmed at his condition. "Poor boy." She slipped in the back of the wagon and made a space for Max to put him down. "Cordelia, you drive the wagon and I'll take care of this child."

Duke whined and climbed onto the seat beside me.

We took off. I wondered how many more collapsed go-backers we might find and whether we would have room for all of them.

Up ahead, I saw five wagons with exhausted-looking horses and mules stopped by the trail. Folks were standing by what looked like an open grave.

"Cordelia," Miz Wilma called. "Stop and ask if they might know this boy."

I nodded and guided the wagon toward the group of ten mourners, including a woman and a boy about nine. One of the men was saying a prayer. I stopped the mules a few feet from them and waited until the prayer was over. They picked up shovels and started filling in the grave.

One of the men walked over to our wagon, eyeing me as though he suspected I was up to no good. "What do you want?"

"We found a boy about fourteen passed out on the trail. Thought you might know him," I said.

The man took off his hat and wiped sweat from his forehead. "Could be Jake. He said he needed a few minutes to rest, and he'd catch up." The man shook his head. "That's his pa we just buried. He doesn't have anyone else traveling with us."

His tone suggested he didn't want to take on Jake's care. "What about his property?" I asked. "We're taking him to the nearest place he can get help. Does one of those wagons and pair of mules belong to him and his father?"

"Well," the man said, reluctant, like he didn't want to give anything up.

"Miz Wilma," I called, "his name's Jake. Ask him what belongings he has with the group he was traveling with." I hesitated, hating to deliver bad news in a shout, but I didn't want to take my eyes off someone who had left a boy to die of thirst on the trail. "His Pa is the one that's being buried. We need to take his possessions with us."

Max came up beside me on his horse and sat with his hand on his leg next to his gun. I figured he sensed trouble too.

Miz Wilma came to the front of the wagon and peered out between the flaps. "Jake says his wagon is the one with 'Busted' written on the front flap. The whole outfit, including the mules, are his pa's."

The man puffed up and scowled. "How do I know this boy's Jake? How do I know he said anything?"

Miz Wilma shook her head. "You're welcome to come have a look. We'll see if he recognizes you."

The man stomped to the back of the wagon and climbed up to peer inside.

I heard Jake's voice, faint. "Hey, Wayne. They just said my pa died."

"He did. We buried him proper. I guess you're riding with these folks."

"Guess so."

"We'll leave your rig with them then. We wasted enough time here."

It was all I could do not to tell this "Wayne" off. They'd "wasted time" burying a man? I guess that showed what we were dealing with.

I guessed Wayne thought it was a waste because we showed up with Jake, and now he couldn't go off with Jake's gear.

Max rode over to Jake's wagon, tied his horse on the back and climbed onto the wagon box. He moved out, and I followed, my eyes on the group as we passed, wondering if we would have trouble down the trail, glad there was a stage station about ten miles ahead and hoping we wouldn't have a skirmish later. These go-backers might be behind us the rest of the way home.

I looked over my shoulder to see what was going on inside our wagon. Duke and Miz Wilma were looking out the back, Miz Wilma gripping her shotgun, prepared for trouble.

It was almost dark when we reached Station 22. Jake had roused some and was able to sit up in the wagon and eat the oatmeal and molasses Miz Wilma fixed for us. The food was getting monotonous, but one thing I had learned about traveling was to eat when you could and not complain. Anything was better than nothing.

Max took care of the livestock, but it was going to be costly now that we had two extra mules to water and feed. I dug into the money I had saved, wondering if it had been a good thing to bring Jake's wagon with us. Not only was there the extra expense, but the men in the other group were enemies now, thinking we had taken something they already saw as theirs.

Once he ate, Jake fell back to sleep.

"He'll likely be out for another day or so," Miz Wilma said. "It will take time for him to heal."

"I wonder if he's got family anywhere," I said.

"Hope he does. He's a little young to be on his own. Then again, there's lots his age that are these days."

With Jake sleeping in the wagon, I bedded down on the ground on the opposite side of the fire from Max.

***

By the next night, Jake felt well enough to join us at the campfire. We hadn't seen anything of the group that buried his father since leaving them, but Max was convinced that Wayne, the man who wanted to know why we'd stopped, might still show up. Jake agreed. He believed Wayne had poisoned him and his father.

Jake sat clutching his cup of broth, sipping now and then, telling us his story. "Wayne's wagon broke down. He couldn't fix the axle, so Father let him ride with us. Father and I were as healthy as anyone in the group. Then we both started feeling poorly, got the runs. We traded off walking. Father was weak and couldn't go far. That morning, I couldn't rouse him from bed. I went out to find help and Wayne came. He'd been helping us for a couple of days, and I was glad to see him. He gave me something to eat, and by the time I finished it, I was feeling sickly. I went off a hundred yards so as not to offend the women, found a mesquite bush for cover. By the time I was ready to go back, I heard them calling to leave. Wayne was driving our wagon. I hurried to reach them but fell and couldn't get up. That must be where you found me."

He finished the rest of his broth. "There was no reason we should be sick when no one else was. Wayne wanted our wagon and mules. If you hadn't helped me, he'd have them." He glanced around at each of us. "Do you think he might do anything to the others?"

Max shook his head. "Seems like that would be a big chance to take. When the folks who help him take sick and die, and someone else gives him a ride and starts getting sick, everyone would get suspicious. Didn't he have a horse or mule?"

"He did, but he gambled them away one night when he was drunk."

Miz Wilma rested her coffee cup on her lap. "Man sounds like trouble."

"For sure, I won't be going around helping anyone again," Jake said.

"Now don't let this experience close your heart to others," Miz Wilma said. "Where would you be if we'd took that attitude? You'd be lying back on the trail, dead, that's where." She swallowed and studied him. "I been going up and down this trail for years now, helping folks that needs it. A couple of times, I got robbed, believe it or not, but you see I don't have much, so there wasn't much they could take. But the thing I could have let them take that would have hurt most was my caring about others. I had a choice in that, and I decided to trust and help others."

I put an arm around Miz Wilma's shoulders. "That's why I'm here. Miz Wilma came to my rescue when I was alone on the trail. She bandaged my feet and gave me a ride. Back in Denver City, when I saw she was hurt, I knew I had to help her. Then we saw you and had to stop for you, too. We hope you'll do that for someone who needs you someday."

Max had been listening and put in his opinion. "Just keep an eye on those you help. They'll slip up and let you know what they're about if you pay attention."

Miz Wilma nodded. "Being helpful doesn't mean you have to be gullible."

About this time, Duke sidled up to Jake and nudged his hand, looking for attention.

Miz Wilma laughed. "If the dog likes someone, it's a good sign."

Jake patted Duke. "Guess I'll have to get a dog."

We all laughed.

17) A BLOSSOMING ROMANCE

Lucy

Getting Pa and Miss Carstairs together wasn't as easy as I'd thought it would be. He seemed to be slow taking the hint. Wondering if Mrs. Collins might have any suggestions, I stopped by her boardinghouse the next afternoon and waited impatiently while she instructed the kitchen staff on the menus for the day. When at last she was finished, we sat at one of the dining room tables, and I told her what I'd done so far. Eager for her opinion, I leaned toward her. "What should I do next?"

She squeezed my hand. "I'm not sure you should do anything, Lucy. It seems like you've set the stage for them to get together if they want to, and your father has never been shy about going after something or someone he wants. He certainly wasn't shy about asking me to marry him."

"Maybe he doesn't know he wants her yet? Or maybe he's shy now after getting turned down. He is pretty prideful."

"Hmmm. Your Pa shy? I suppose he could be although it doesn't sound like the Hiram I know."

I frowned. "And don't love."

She set her jaw. "We're friends."

I'd heard that before. "So why don't you think Miss Carstairs is perfect for Pa?"

"I didn't say she wasn't. But, truthfully, she just came to town. We don't know anything about her."

"We know she's related to the Fletchers, sings in the church choir, has a good alto voice, is unmarried, and looking to be married. What else is there?"

"Will they get along? Do they want the same things in life?"

I sighed. "I suppose that means she has to want to have a baby every year until the house is full of boys."

Mrs. Collins nodded. "That would be a good start."

"We're never going to find out until we get them together."

"So invite her to Sunday dinner."

I groaned. "So I can ruin another meal in front of company?"

"You'll get better with practice, dear. The same can be said of matchmaking."

"You think I need practice? I was hoping this one would do it. Besides, I haven't seen any other eligible women around town."

"Others will come. Like that new teacher we'll hire. If we hire a woman, of course."

I left the boardinghouse shaking my head. If Mrs. Collins wouldn't help, I'd just have to figure out something on my own.

Head held high, I marched down the street to the general store. Sunday dinner was all the advice I had to go on, so Sunday dinner it was.

***

On Sunday, I stood with the choir, sharing a hymnbook with Miss Carstairs, trying to see if Pa was paying any attention to her.

He seemed to be looking at her, but he might be looking at me, trying to decide if my singing was passable or was embarrassing him. I was so busy trying to figure out what he was thinking that I lost the line. Miss Carstairs put her finger on the place in the hymn book.

So here I was, making another bad impression.

With the last hymn over, the service ended with a prayer, and we all drifted toward the front door, following Reverend Sherwood, holding back to let those in the pews file into the central aisle.

Reverend Sherwood's wife joined him, and the two stood shaking hands with each person as they exited the church, thanking them for coming.

Once outside, I guided Miss Carstairs to our buggy.

She was impressed. There was only one other buggy at the church, and it belonged to Mayor Tompkins.

Ambrose came out, and I introduced them. He greeted her and

gave her a hand up. She settled in the front seat, and Ambrose and I climbed in back. Pa was still talking to Mayor Tompkins. I wanted to throw a rock at him to get his attention, but I thought better of it. I had a meal warming in the oven, just enough heat from the coals to keep it warm without over cooking it—if we got home like we should.

The minutes dragged on, maybe five, and Miss Carstairs began to fidget and talk to Ambrose about the furniture he might make for the house and praise him for what a good job he had done on the stonework. This was not going well. I didn't want her fastening on my brother, who was years too young for her and had probably never even kissed a girl, just like I'd never kissed a boy.

Finally, Pa shook hands with the mayor and ambled to the buggy. "Sorry to keep you waiting, Miss Carstairs," he said. "Pressing town business sometimes can't wait for tomorrow."

"I do understand, Mr. Pierce. Lucy has told me you are a founding member of the town and on the council. You must be very civic-minded."

"We've done a lot to build the town. It's grown, even with the recent Panic across the country the last couple of years." He glanced back at me. "I saw that fidgeting you were doing. You need to learn business comes first."

I wanted to say he needed to learn that a dinner warming in the oven comes first, but I held my tongue. I was getting to be just like Cordelia, thinking before I spoke. It was not a trait I liked.

Pa snapped the whip, and the horse started off toward home.

When we got to the house, I raced for the kitchen and opened the oven. The baked chicken was dry. So was the stuffing. The gravy had thickened to a paste, and the apple cobbler's crust had blackened around the edge of the pan. I buried my face in my hands. Another ruined meal.

Ambrose put a hand on my shoulder. "What's wrong?"

"It's all overdone. Where's Pa? He's going to be mad again."

"He and Miss Carstairs are in the dining room looking at those wall covering samples. Hey, let's try to fix this. Maybe rub some butter on the chicken and stir some water into the gravy to thin it. You can serve the cobbler with cream. It will be fine."

I stared at my brother. "How did you get so smart about cooking?"

"Who do you think did it before you came?"

My brother, the one with all the skills, and me with none. I wasn't wife material. I was barely person material. I hoped I was better at matchmaking than I was at cooking.

***

While the butter didn't do much for the chicken, Ambrose's suggestions to thin the gravy and pour cream on the cobbler saved the meal. Pa seemed less at ease pouring out criticisms in front of Miss Carstairs. I hoped that was because he saw her as a possible wife and didn't want to scare her off with bad manners.

Miss Carstairs gave Pa a couple of compliments, and he got started on his reputation of making the best axes anywhere and his ambitions for rising in government if Kansas ever got to be a state. "Just one delay after another," he said. "But we'll get there, and it will be as a free state, regardless of how much trouble those proslavery ruffians give us. I stood up to them and have the scar to prove it."

Miss Carstairs widened her eyes. "My cousins said something about how those horrible men wrecked your shop and your home."

"Scared my wife. Probably made her illness worse with all the worry and fear. We lost her and the child not long after. My burn and broken ribs hadn't healed yet."

It was the first I'd heard Pa speak of Ma's death in casual conversation. He said the words about losing her like her loss meant nothing to him. It was hard to hear him talk that way. I began gathering the plates and took them away. Then I dished the cobbler into bowls and brought a pitcher of cream to the table. I waited anxiously as the pitcher went around and Pa and Miss Carstairs took their first bites.

Miss Carstairs swallowed and put the spoon down. "This is delicious, Lucy. Perhaps you'll give me your recipe."

"Be proud to," I said, wondering if letting it bake dry should be part of the instructions.

She turned her attention back to Pa. "Do you own much land?"

"Just the hundred and sixty acres. There might come a time when I can buy out a few of the other small farms around here. Some folks aren't cut out for farming. Now Ambrose, here, can grow about anything he plants."

Ambrose smiled at the praise. "Thanks, Pa, but that corn didn't do too well last year."

130

Pa nodded. "Almost anything then."

"What do you raise?" Miss Carstairs asked.

Pa laid his spoon aside. "Mostly food for the table. We have a cow, a dozen chickens, two pigs and a new litter. Then there's the garden for potatoes and such. Lucy's taking care of those things now so Ambrose can spend more time working at the stable in town."

"You're lucky to have two such industrious children."

"There's two more girls. They're in Westport with their aunts, getting an education. I reckon they'll be back here in a year or two if we get the school going with a steady teacher instead of these women that get married at the end of every term. I talked with a man teacher over at Ft. Riley, but he likes where he is."

"How old are your other two girls?"

Pa frowned at me like he wanted me to say something.

"Ella is nine and Jennie is seven," I said.

"I'd hoped for more sons," Pa said.

"You're still young," Miss Carstairs threw in. "Perhaps you'll marry and have more children, and some of those will be sons."

Pa gave her a look like she'd turned in an application and he was considering her for the job. "Let me show you around the place," he said.

Eyes gleaming, she replied, "I'd love that."

After the two of them went outside, Ambrose frowned and glared at me. "What are you doing?"

"Finding Pa a wife, so he'll quit trying to find a husband for me."

"Finding one won't keep him from doing the other. And who is she? How do we know we want her living in the house with us, taking Ma's place?"

Taking Ma's place? I hadn't thought of it that way.

That afternoon when I settled down to write to Ella and Jennie, I decided not to tell them about the matchmaking part of the week. I wrote that I had joined the choir at church and to be sure to tell Aunt Hilda because she would be happy, and that I met Miss Carstairs from the general store and she was helping me choose wall coverings and draperies to get the house ready for company.

**

Romance seemed to be blossoming between Pa and Miss Carstairs. Now that I'd lit the fire, it was getting out of control. I'd thought about a long courtship of at least a few months. Maybe a

Christmas wedding, but they both were moving fast, almost inseparable since Sunday dinner.

I no longer had any say in decorating the house. Miss Carstairs directly consulted Pa each step of the way. She ordered the wallpaper. She showed Ambrose the dining room furniture he was to replicate and ordered the wood to make it.

In the midst of all the courting and decorating, Pa still found time to locate a prospective husband for me. Doctor Clem White from Junction City was on that city's council, a thirtyish man with two small children, his wife having died of cholera. He was a friend of Doc Sloan's family and had come west because of the need for a doctor in that town.

He was all right although he seemed to be a better match for Miss Carstairs than for me. However, due to my actions, Miss Carstairs was already taken.

Miss Carstairs planned a dinner Sunday after church to introduce me to Doctor White and his children, two rambunctious boys. It was July 3, hot and sticky. Miss Carstairs had Ambrose set up a table outside with long planks and sawhorses. Planks across nail kegs made up the benches for sitting.

I was inside frying chicken and baking bread. Two peach pies were cooling on the worktable. Glancing out the window, I saw Pa and Miss Carstairs sitting in the shade with Doctor White, relaxing with glasses of water. I wiped sweat from my forehead and turned my attention back to the cooking. I had learned that for everything to turn out right, I must keep an eye on the food. For just a moment, I considered burning everything. That might discourage Doctor White from thinking of me as wife material. I also wished I didn't look older than my age. I'd always been so proud when strangers mistook me for older than Cordelia and flirted with me instead of her, but now I wished I looked thirteen, the age I was. Sure, I'd be fourteen in a couple of months, but if I looked younger, maybe Doctor White or any other man Pa considered suitable would think I was too young.

The bread was done. I took it out of the oven and smoothed butter on the top to keep the crust soft.

Ambrose came in and watched me. "You're getting better at cooking."

"Lucky me," I said. "Now I get to do cooking for the guests Miss Carstairs invites."

I set the bread aside and started turning the chicken. "Ambrose, please take the baked potatoes out of the oven."

He grabbed two hot-pads and opened the oven door. The blast of heat left me wishing for a cool breeze like the ones Pa, Miss Carstairs, and Doctor White were probably enjoying.

Ambrose grinned. "I told you matchmaking wasn't a good idea."

"Thank you for that." I glared at him. "How did you know?"

"While you were spending time with people your own age, going to school, and working for Aunt Hannah, I was here watching what happens when people want or need to find a husband or wife. People die, or leave, or don't come west like they promised. Children are wanted, Pa's dynasty thing. When someone who has children marries someone who doesn't, and new babies come, things happen. Girls, especially, have a hard time if boys come along."

"Why? I'm here. I'm Pa's daughter. Doesn't that count for something?"

"Only if you marry well. If Pa marries Miss Carstairs, and it looks like he will, then you are no longer the lady of the house."

"It feels like she already is," I grumbled.

"This is nothing. Wait until they marry. Then you will be a servant: you'll do all the work, and she'll get all the credit."

I pushed back hair straggling around my face. "That's already happening."

"If you don't want to be a servant, you'll have to get married so you'll have your own house."

"That's just trading masters. Look out the window at those hooligans of Doctor White's. I don't want to be their stepmother. I'm not ready to be anyone's mother, step or otherwise."

Ambrose shook his head. "I don't think you have a choice."

I sighed. "Aunt Hannah said I could come back to live with her if things didn't work out."

"Pa won't let you go."

"I know," I snapped. "You've said it often enough."

He shook his head and put a lid on the pan with the potatoes to keep them warm. "I'll take these to the table. It looks like everything is almost done."

He banged the door on his way out.

Sorry for snapping at him, my only ally, I dished up the chicken and carried it outside.

When I set the platter on the table, Miss Carstairs leaned forward and smiled. "Lucy is becoming such a fine cook, Doctor White. Wait until you taste her peach pie. She's won prizes for it."

"Only one prize," I said, "and that was a tie."

"For first place," she said.

"Boys," Doctor White called. "Come have a seat. It's time for a prayer and our meal."

They came running, two boys of seven and eight, lively, pushing each other, squabbling over who would sit next to Miss Carstairs, the center of even these small males' attention.

We bowed our heads and Pa said the prayer. Then he passed the food around. We each took servings, Ambrose helping the younger boys with theirs. Once again, my brother seemed years older than his true age, someone who would make an excellent husband and father. I wondered how he would choose from all the young ladies I was sure would be lined up wanting to marry him. But then, we did live in an area of the country with a woman shortage. If I wanted to escape marriage, I needed to find a way back to Westport and Aunt Hannah.

It wasn't that I never wanted to marry. I just didn't want to do it right now. Surely, I could wait to be a wife and mother until I was at least Cordelia's age. I was gradually facing a fear I hadn't known I had. Dying in childbirth. So many young women had, including my own mother. I thought of Ma seeing so many of her babies die after such hope for their lives, and then to die herself. The possibility that the same fate awaited me made me ill. I was not ready for that life. I wanted some years to enjoy before having babies raised my chances of dying. Surely, another four or five years wasn't too much to ask. On the other hand, Ambrose was right. I would spend it being a servant to Miss Carstairs. What was the advantage in that?

"Lucy," Miss Carstairs said. "I believe you've forgotten to bring out the salt and pepper." She gave me a pointed look.

"Yes, ma'am," I said and hurried to the house to retrieve them.

How could I get out of this mess I'd gotten myself into?

***

While everyone else took a walk around the farm, I washed dishes and tidied up the kitchen. Then I pumped well water and wet a cloth to cool my face and neck. I heard Pa and his guests coming toward the house, Miss Carstairs's voice above the rest, saying "Let me show you the parlor and our plans for it."

"Our plans?" I was no longer a part of "our" even though I was the one who first talked to her about it. I had to admit to being jealous. I wanted Pa to think I was smart and capable and worth having around. Truth, though, if he thought that, he'd just try that much harder to find me a "suitable" husband.

Whether I was a disaster or a gem, I was doomed to marry younger than I wanted. Doctor White's boys whooped past me into the house, slamming the door in front of Pa's face. I saw his cheeks get red like he wanted to yell at them, but he kept his temper in. After all, he didn't want to spoil my matrimonial chances with the doctor.

He glanced at me. "Are you coming, Lucy? You're neglecting our guest."

"I had dishes to finish," I said. "I can join you now."

I tagged along at the end of the group as we entered the parlor. Miss Carstairs settled onto the window seat and held up a catalogue. "We've ordered these easy chairs and lamps. Ambrose is making the tables. Such a talented boy."

Pa nodded and clamped a hand on Ambrose's shoulder. "He certainly is. Helped me cut and lay the stone for this house."

It was more like Pa had helped Ambrose, but I knew Pa didn't see it that way.

"Well, we'd best be getting back to Junction City," Doctor White said. He took my hand. "It was a pleasure to meet you, Miss Pierce. Thank you for the fine meal." Releasing me, he continued, "Perhaps you will be visiting Junction City soon. We have several excellent shops. Being near the fort and on the stage route has encouraged business. The Independence Day celebration is tomorrow. Perhaps, you'll all come."

Pa's face flushed. "We have a celebration right here in Hidden Springs. As a councilman, I can't be running off to some other town." The chill in his voice told me Doctor White had just gone down a peg or two in Pa's mind.

Doctor White seemed to guess his mistake. "Of course, not, Hiram. It slipped my mind. Forgive me."

Pa forgive someone for forgetting he was important? Not likely. I saw a way to get rid of future suitors—just get them to say something that showed they didn't realize how important Pa was, and he'd cross them off my prospective husband list.

***

Independence Day was Monday, so no one had to worry about frivolity on the Sabbath. There was a picnic and speeches on the school grounds. They were going to announce the new teacher and the plans to build a town hall. Pa had suggested Ambrose for the town hall job. Ordinarily, someone Ambrose's age wouldn't have a chance, but all anyone had to do was look at our house to see he knew how to work with stone.

I had baked one of my now famous peach pies and set it out on the long sawhorse plank table with the others. I had also fixed a large dish of green beans with onions and salt pork and a loaf of bread. Everything had turned out perfectly, which meant I looked like good wife material for someone. The only salvation I had was that there was a shortage of eligible suitors. There were plenty of single men around, and I could have had my pick if I was doing the picking. But since it was up to Pa, the immediate supply in Hidden Springs had been exhausted. However, as I had seen with Doctor White, he wasn't above bringing in outside possibilities. As long as I remembered to work them into saying something less than respectful to Pa, I was safe.

I wished I could join Willy and Susan strolling around the games. Three boys about my age took turns showing their skill at knocking a bowling pin off a table with a baseball while younger children skipped rope and played "Drop the Handkerchief." Later, there would be a three-legged race. I was supposed to run it with Ambrose, the only person my age I ever got to talk to, at least in the open.

There had been the day I'd run into Willy fishing at the creek and talked to him for almost an hour. Sitting there on the creek bank, reminiscing about Westport and my sisters and how much I missed them and listening to Willy's stories of all the crazy pranks he had pulled on Susan and she had pulled on him, I had a chance to laugh again, to remember what being happy felt like. Then a fish hit Willy's line and broke the spell of our chat. I hurried home, desperate to catch up on my chores before Pa showed up and demanded to know why they weren't done.

The mayor blew a whistle to let us know it was time to eat. We all bowed our heads while Reverend Sherwood said the blessing. Then we lined up to serve food to others or fix a plate for ourselves. Before long, we sat at makeshift tables or on blankets spread on the ground. After we finished the last of our food, Mayor Tompkins was at the podium again, saying he was proud to see us all here and how we hoped it wouldn't be much longer before Kansas became a state instead of a territory. He said building strong communities would help the Congress make that decision and that men like Hiram Pierce were responsible for the strength of Hidden Springs. "And now Hiram has a few words to say."

Pa got up and thanked the mayor for the kind words. Seeing Pa up there, everyone respecting him and waiting to hear what he had to say made me proud to be his daughter. It was the feeling I'd had when I got the letter that he wanted me to come home. He looked handsome and prosperous in his suit. He was clean-shaven and his hair was still as black as mine. Well, maybe not completely. Someone standing up close, like Miss Carstairs often did, could see a few gray strands in all the black. Still, they made him look distinguished, like he'd been around long enough to know a thing or two about how the world worked.

Pa took off his top hat and placed it on a chair behind him, then turned to the crowd.

"Hello, friends and neighbors. Are you all enjoying this fine Independence Day celebration?"

There was a rousing "yes" and a round of clapping.

"What? Is that a sign of the fun you're having? Can we hear that again a little stronger?"

There was laughter from the crowd, a louder "yes" and clapping, whistling, and stomping feet.

"That's more like it." He paused and looked around. "Let's have another round for the ladies and all the good food they prepared."

Everyone responded with another wave of applause.

"Those ladies include my lovely daughter, Lucy, and my bride-to-be, Miss Ava Carstairs."

My mouth dropped open. This was the first official word of a marriage.

Ambrose leaned forward and whispered. "See what you did. Now we're stuck with her."

The crowd settled down, and Pa continued his speech. "We're planning a fall wedding. And now, with the social announcements out of the way, I'll get down to business. We have hired a teacher. He comes highly recommended by an educator at Ft. Riley and previous employers at a public school in Boston." He motioned to a man sitting at the end of the line of men to the left of the podium. "Mr. Frank Derryberry, come on up and say hello."

The tall, lanky man rose and stepped up beside Pa, and they shook hands. "Mr. Derryberry will be staying with me and my family until he finds more permanent accommodations after the coming school year."

I groaned. Another person to clean up after and do laundry for.

Ambrose chuckled and whispered in my ear. "So how does Mrs. Lucy Derryberry sound to you?"

I glared at him. Of course, that was Pa's plan. And with Mr. Derryberry in the house, there wouldn't be room for Ella and Jennie to come. Not that I wanted them to anymore. Well, maybe a little.

I looked down at my empty plate, my stomach churning, glad I had finished my food.

There were more speeches, one about the new city building to be built. "My son, Ambrose, who you all know was apprenticed to a fine stone mason and did a major part of the building of my home, will be in charge of the construction. Ambrose, come up here and say a few words."

Ambrose groaned and trudged to the podium. I smiled, knowing how much he hated speaking to crowds. It served him right. Mrs. Derryberry, indeed.

18) THERE WAS NOTHING WE COULD DO

Cordelia

The days passed with a kind of monotony. One late afternoon, we were three or four miles from Station 14, hot, tired, ready for some cool well water. We had seen buffalo for the last couple of days, a few at first, and then huge herds crossing in front of us. An hour had gone by without seeing any of the huge beasts when the quiet of the day was broken by a series of shots fired followed by a rumbling. The ground shook.

Miz Wilma straightened. For the first time since I'd known her, she had true fear in her eyes. "Stampede."

In the distance a fast-moving sea of brown charged toward us.

We brought the wagons together in a V and crouched on the ground as the first buffalo emerged from the blur of the herd. "Shoot the lead animals," Miz Wilma shouted. "The others will go around."

Max and Jake took up their rifles and began shooting. Two animals fell, then three, but the herd wasn't doing much direction changing. They were all around us, crashing into Miz Wilma's wagon until the frame broke. Duke came flying out, yipping, plunging to the ground, running blindly into the herd.

"Duke," Miz Wilma cried, limping toward him.

"Miz Wilma, come back!" I scrambled to my feet to chase after her, but Max grabbed my arm and pulled me to him. I struggled to get loose, but he held on tight.

"You can't, you can't," he said.

Duke stood frozen and shivering as Miz Wilma struggled toward him, a huge buffalo coming at him full speed. Miz Wilma was a foot from Duke when the buffalo knocked her to the ground and trampled them both. I screamed and buried my face in Max's chest while Jake sobbed and kept firing.

Shouts came from behind the buffalo. A dozen or so Indians rode at the end of the herd, firing arrows. Several of the animals dropped.

The danger was over, and Miz Wilma was dead. Max let go of me. I ran to her, fell to my knees, and pressed my face to her mangled chest. "No. Oh, no."

Max knelt beside me and tried to pull me away.

An Indian rode up. At the sight of Miz Wilma's trampled body, his face dissolved in grief, and he let out a soul-piercing cry that matched my own anguish.

Women followed behind him, faces saddened at the sight, Miz Wilma's name whispered from one to another, voices keening her loss, mourning the woman who had helped so many of their people over the years.

The brave who had first come to us spoke in halting English. "White men started this stampede with rifles. They rode on and we, hunting buffalo, followed the animals." He looked at Miz Wilma's body. "We must bury her with honor."

"And Duke," I said. "She would want Duke with her."

The women set about butchering the buffalo while Max and Jake lifted Miz Wilma's body onto boards from the broken wagon. One of the water barrels was still intact. I dampened a cloth and began washing away the mud and blood from her body. But the sight of her crushed face overwhelmed me. My stomach revolted, and I turned away, retching, emptying my breakfast onto the sandy soil.

One woman approached. "They have sent me because I speak your language," she said. "I will help. Is she your mother?"

"She was everyone's mother," I said.

"Yes." She took the cloth from me and continued bathing Miz Wilma's body.

Max stayed with me, holding me close, while Jake gathered the scattered belongings from Miz Wilma's demolished wagon.

Once the woman finished bathing Miz Wilma, she asked, "Are there special clothes for her burial?"

I stepped carefully through the broken pieces of the wagon and found a trunk containing some of her belongings. Inside, I found a pale yellow dress of homespun and a small box that held a butterfly-shaped silver brooch. They seemed so different from the buckskins she usually wore, items from a past life, but still hers. I wished I could have known more of her story, but I had been too wrapped up in my own to ask. Now it was too late.

I figured the clothes and the brooch had to be special to her, so I handed them to the Indian woman. She enlisted three other women, and they dressed Miz Wilma in her burial clothes.

"We need blankets to wrap her in," the woman said.

I found two blankets and offered the buffalo robe she slept in at night.

The woman smiled and, with the help of her friends, placed Duke at Miz Wilma's waist. They wrapped the two tightly together, the blankets first and then the buffalo hide on the outside, bound securely with leather strips.

While the women prepared Miz Wilma's body, Jake dug her grave. The Indian brave who had spoken to me joined him with a shovel Max provided. Except for that time, Max stayed by my side, hugging me, patting my shoulder, trying to comfort me, but nothing could stop the ache in my heart.

Jake came and leaned the shovels against the wagon. "We're ready," he said.

I pressed away from Max's chest and forced myself to look at the open grave. Gathered around it was the small band of Indians who had left their work of butchering the buffalo to attend the burial. Four of them stepped forward and carried her to the grave where they placed her on a buffalo hide and lowered her carefully into her last resting place. A wail that I knew was a death song commenced among them. When it ended, there was a moment of silence. Then Max said a prayer, and I managed a few words about her goodness and care for all.

When the time came to fill in the grave, I could not look as Jake and Max shoveled dirt. The Indian woman squeezed my hand.

In the distance, we heard rumbling and saw dust flying. A stage appeared on the horizon as Jake poured the last shovelful of dirt on the grave. The stage driver pulled to a stop and came over, glancing at the gathering of Indians.

"What happened?"

"A buffalo stampede," I said. On impulse, I asked, "Did you know of Miz Wilma?"

"Yes." He looked at the grave. "Is she the one—?"

I nodded.

"Do you need help here?"

"No, but tell them at the station we'll be along later tonight."

"Yes, ma'am."

Casting a wary look at our company, he hurried back to the stage and left us.

Then the Indians brought stones they had picked up and placed them on Miz Wilma's grave, covering it as protection from wild animals.

The Indian woman had gathered many of Miz Wilma's salves and healing herbs. "There is much medicine here," she said.

"And none of us knows how to use it," I replied. "If you do, I am sure she would want you to have it."

"Thank you." She bundled the medicines into a pouch and joined her people in preparing the buffalo meat.

We packed Miz Wilma's belongings onto Ready and Waiting since we would be traveling in Jake's wagon now. Jake's mules and Max's horse had also survived. It was dark except for the moonlight that was bright enough for us to follow the wagon trail left by the stage.

We had not eaten since midday, but no one had an appetite. We rode in silence, Jake driving, Max on his horse, the distance between us and Miz Wilma's grave growing.

I thought of Ma, of how I hadn't seen her grave since the day we buried her. I sighed, a whole-body sigh that ended with me shaking. There was so much loss in the world, and it always seemed to be the good people dying. If someone had to die, why couldn't it be someone like Hiram who was so hateful? Or that Bob Sims? Or Wayne, who had left Jake to die. I remembered what Miz Wilma said about everyone having a story, but I didn't care about their stories. I just wanted Miz Wilma back. I wanted my mother back. I wanted Lucy to understand my story so we could be loving sisters again.

***

We were at Station 12. If all went well, I might make Hidden Springs by mid-July. I said as much to Max.

He frowned. "Why are you going back there? You hate your stepfather."

"Lucy's there. I have to make sure she's okay. She had such rosy pictures of what life with her father would be. I'm sure they were dashed."

"What about you, Cordelia? Did you have hopes about Quinn? How did that turn out for you?"

"I always hoped for good things. I didn't believe any of those hopes would come true, but they did. Not right away, though. The day we met, it was awkward with nothing but the acknowledgement that I was his daughter. The next day, when Bob Sims stopped me as I was leaving, yelling at me and acting like he was going to pull me off Ready, Quinn showed up and rescued me. Then he stayed with me until I reached Miz Wilma."

Saying her name brought tears to my eyes. It had been three days since we buried her and Duke in the middle of that desolate stretch of land that held so many other graves. The thought of the number of buffalo hooves that would tromp over it in the future made me shiver. "She approved of Quinn. And when I said I was traveling with her because she needed my help, he said it was dangerous but didn't try to talk me out of it. That he could be my father and not try to tell me what I had to do was what made me certain he was the best kind of father for me." I glanced at Max. "Of course, I didn't know then that he was going to send you to look out for me."

"Lucky for you he did. You might have been trampled otherwise."

"I wanted to save her."

"I know. Wanting to save someone can cause you to lose your own life."

"Are you thinking of your sister Claire and how you tried to save her from that womanizing gambler, Lucky?"

"Yes."

"How is Claire now?"

"Married to a shopkeeper. Respectable. So what I did worked. If I hadn't stopped Lucky, she would have gone with him and ruined her life. Probably become one of those soiled doves."

I leaned in and whispered so no one could hear. "But you'll be on the run forever, never knowing when someone will recognize you. Her life is saved at the cost of your own."

His mouth was next to my cheek, his breath warm in my ear. "It's been four years, and no one has recognized me yet."

"But they could, any time, and you would be at the end of a rope with a broken neck."

He drew back and looked in my eyes. "Is that why you ignore what's between us?"

"Yes."

He sighed. "I thought it might be because I hadn't made my feelings clear."

"You didn't make them clear to me. My Aunt Hannah, who hasn't even met you, told me."

"What?"

"When she was taking me back to Hidden Springs, we passed Pawnee, and I told her about you kidnapping me and thinking you were responsible for slowing me down, so you made sure I was safe by following me all the way to Westport. She said you had to like me because no one takes those chances just to be nice."

"She's pretty smart."

"You have no idea how smart. She said I liked you, too, and she had just made me realize it."

His eyes gleamed. "So you do?"

"Yes, but nothing can come of it. You will never be free of the past."

He picked up a rock and turned it in his fingers, the light in his eyes gone. "I should turn myself in."

Alarmed, I mouthed the words "And hang?"

"Maybe not. I was protecting my sister's honor."

"You'd already shot Lucky in the arm, and he didn't draw his gun when you shot him the second time." I hissed. "Claire wasn't even there."

He shook his head and tossed the pebble. "I can have hopes, too."

"And they can turn just as bad as I'm sure Lucy's have."

"What if you're wrong?"

"Then I'm happy for her and my little sisters."

Jake came running. "Get ready for trouble. Those fellows over there are gambling and drinking, and one guy's losing his grubstake."

I glanced at the group of six crouched on a blanket and throwing dice. "It's the stationmaster's job to handle whatever trouble comes."

"The stationmaster is the one winning."

Max jerked his head to one side. "Then the best thing to do is to stay away and let them work things out."

"But—."

Max tried to explain. "Jake, the stationmaster is pretty much the law here. It's his place. If there's a fight, it's those passing through who will get the blame. If you want to get back to your family in the States, stay out of it."

I chipped in. "Sometimes, there's nothing you can do. There was nothing I could do for Miz Wilma besides getting killed trying. She wouldn't have wanted that. And after all the hard work she put in bringing you back from the brink of death, she wouldn't want you to squander the life she saved by getting involved in other folks' business."

Max pointed to a spot near the fire. "Have a seat, Jake, and talk for a spell before we turn in and turn our backs on trouble."

Jake blew out a breath and stared at the men shouting around the dice. "Okay," he said and settled cross-legged on the ground beside us. "What were you all talking about?"

"Sisters," I said. "Do you have any?"

"One," he said. "She's back east with my grandmother."

"All the more reason for you to stay right here and not get involved with those gamblers."

***

A gunshot woke me. Across the dying coals of the fire, I saw Jake rise up on his elbow. Max grabbed his arm and whispered something. Jake lay back down.

I pulled my blanket tighter, wondering who was dead and why. I thought we should do something, and I figured Jake felt the same. He seemed to be struggling with the same things I did. What could I do and would it matter? I supposed Miz Wilma would have tried, but Aunt Hannah would have said to consider what might happen if I let my cry for justice outweigh concern for my safety and what I might do in the long run to keep things like killing from happening. It was the same talk I'd been having with Max earlier.

I chased the pros and cons of butting in for at least an hour before I fell back to sleep.

In the morning, we learned the angry gambler had waited until he believed everyone was sleeping and sneaked into the stationmaster's house, trying to find the stash of money. But he was caught in the act of stealing it and shot in the kitchen area of the cabin.

After finishing our breakfast of oatmeal, molasses, and coffee, we went on our way. We were still ten days from Hidden Springs. The closer we got, the more I worried about Lucy.

We traveled without incident for seven days. The grass grew thicker, water flowed in the streams, and the prairie was alive with birds, rabbits, and prairie dogs. Max and Jake went hunting, and we feasted on rabbit.

Then a huge windstorm blew across the prairie. We covered our heads and those of the animals to protect eyes and noses from the dirt. Hunkering in the wagon, the canvas top billowing and snapping in the wind, we prayed the gusts wouldn't blow us over. When at last, the breeze died, we crept out to see the trail had vanished beneath the dirt. The sun was directly overhead. Our sense of direction was aided by the front of the wagon pointed east. We hitched up the mules and plodded forward, three days to go to Hidden Springs.

19) COMING TOGETHER

Lucy

Mr. Frank Derryberry moved into the spare room the night of the Independence Day picnic. I had wondered at Pa's sudden hurry to furnish it with a bed and chest of drawers the previous week when he had been so focused on the dining room and parlor at the beginning. Now I knew. Silly me for thinking he might have decided to bring my sisters home sooner than planned.

Ambrose carried in his trunk, and Pa showed Mr. Derryberry to the room. While all that was going on, I brought in dishes from the picnic and put them in water before going out to milk the cow. By the time I came in with the milk, the men were at the table, drinking coffee. Mr. Derryberry was smoking a pipe. The smell made my stomach quiver.

"Lucy, bring us more coffee," Pa said.

I hefted the pot and carried it to the table, my eyes tearing as I came closer to the puffs of smoke.

Mr. Derryberry noticed. "My pipe bothers you, miss?"

"It does," I managed to say.

"I'll put it out and smoke outside in the future."

Pa frowned. "Lucy's being rude. You're our guest."

Mr. Derryberry smiled at me. "And as a guest, I don't want to cause discomfort for the lady of the house."

"Thank you," I said.

"Humph," Pa grunted.

I returned to my chores while Pa and Mr. Derryberry talked of the teacher's travels from England to America and of his education and eagerness to begin teaching.

I eavesdropped while I worked, hoping to hear something that would disqualify him as a prospective husband. Getting him to disrespect Pa didn't seem like a good idea because the town needed a teacher for our school. If we lost him at this late date, we might not find another. From what he was saying, he had good qualifications, even having a year at a university before his father's death and the takeover of family finances by his older brother forced him to end his formal education and make his way as a schoolmaster.

Pa talked about being under the direction of older brothers as his reason for relocating to Hidden Springs. I supposed I had heard that story when I was younger, but I hadn't really paid attention then. It was obvious he and Mr. Derryberry were becoming fast friends with their shared family experiences.

As I listened, I evaluated the teacher. He was better than the other two marriage prospects. He had no children, and he was younger, under thirty, had hair, and apparently cared about my physical well-being since he had put out his pipe. But would that consideration last into marriage? Was it something to fool me into believing he cared about my concerns?

Perhaps I would be happy to marry him in five or six years, but not now. I shuddered, the possibility of dying in childbirth filling my mind.

The next morning, I went to the cabin after I finished my chores, something I had gotten into the habit of doing. With all the Independence Day preparations, I had failed to write a Sunday letter to Ella and Jennie, so I carried paper, pen, and ink with me, along with matches to light a candle.

As I entered, I saw a dark shape at the back window where Ma's bed had been. A man. I stepped back. "Who's here?"

"Just I, lass." Mr. Derryberry turned to face me.

"Why are you here?" I asked.

"Seeing what needs to be done. I am to live here once school is in session. I need the quiet for planning lessons and grading my pupils' work."

"Oh." I wanted to tell him he couldn't have this place. It was mine to be close to my mother. But, of course, he could have it. It belonged to Pa. Perhaps that was my incentive. If I married Mr. Derryberry, I could live in the cabin and be close to Ma.

"Do you come here often? Am I intruding?" he asked.

"You're not intruding if Pa says you may live here. I just came to write to my sisters in Westport." I held up the paper and bottle of ink. "For the same reason you will plan lessons here. To have quiet and think."

"You miss your sisters then?"

"Yes. Do you have family still in England?"

"I do. And I write once a month."

"Then you are on good terms?"

"Yes. Why do you ask?"

"What you said last night about your older brothers. You seemed to have the same family situation as Pa, and he can't stand his relatives. They only write when a baby is born or someone dies."

"That's too bad," he said. "Well, I will leave you to your letter writing."

"I didn't mean to rush you off."

"That's all right. I will return in an hour or so with a measuring stick. The area back by the window looks like a good place for a bed."

"Yes, Ma's bed was there."

"And your father?"

I laughed. "His, too, but she was so often ill, it seemed like mostly hers."

"Well, then, I will return later."

When he was gone, I took a seat at the table, probably for the last time here. I touched the locket with Ma's hair in it, sad that another connection was being broken. I felt so close to her here, even closer than at the cemetery. I felt like when I wrote to Ella and Jennie, Ma was in the room, looking over my shoulder. I brought their letters here to read so she could see them too.

Gone. All the losses. I thought of Cordelia and wondered how she was doing in the west, a dangerous land. But Cordelia always seemed to make it through. I wondered how she did it.

***

While I was preparing supper, Mr. Derryberry, who had a subscription to the White Cloud *Kansas Chief*, was pouring over an issue at the kitchen table. Shaking his head, he pointed to an article.

149

"That Greeley fellow of the *Tribune* is still trying to play up the gold discoveries around Pikes Peak. They want to get everyone out there and fleece them for their money." He scanned the page. "The circus is coming to White Cloud, another important news item." He folded the paper and looked at me. "Do you follow the news, Miss Pierce?"

"Not since I left Westport. My Aunt Hannah is a suffragette and big on the news. She gives speeches and goes on demonstrations to get women the vote." I figured such news would put him on warning that I might be of the same mind as my aunt and not a good candidate for wife.

He did not seem upset by the revelation. In fact, he perked up and looked rather excited at the prospect. "And do you also aspire to voting?"

"No, I follow my Aunt Hilda's faith. She is the wife of a minister and has a more traditional view of a woman's sphere."

"I imagine that makes for lively discussions around the dinner table."

"Not really. They don't like each other much and seldom dine together."

"So both your mother's and your father's families are at odds with each other?"

"I had never thought of it, but, yes, that's true. After we moved to Hidden Springs five years ago, we had little contact with either side. It was Cordelia who brought Aunt Hannah back into our lives."

"Cordelia? I don't believe I've heard that name."

Now I'd done it. No one outside immediate family knew she wasn't Pa's daughter. How was I to explain?

"She's my older sister. She went out to the gold fields you were reading about to find a long-lost relative on my mother's side of the family."

"But you said the sides were at war."

"We only have rumors of this one, so all we know is he's looking for gold. I guess if he finds some, my aunt will want him back in the family." That didn't come out quite like I wanted it to. I'd made it sound like Aunt Hannah was greedy and looking for a family member to get part of his money if he made any.

"Well, good luck to the family prospector, but as of June 30, the *Kansas Chief* didn't think he'd have any in spite of what Horace Greeley supposedly said."

Pa came in and saw the newspaper folded on the table. "That thing recent?"

"Only a week old. I received it yesterday afternoon. Would you like to read it?"

"Sure would. Like to see what's happening and if we're getting any closer to being a state."

"There's a story about electing delegates to a convention to write a state constitution." Mr. Derryberry held out the newspaper.

Pa grabbed it. "What page?"

"Two, I believe."

While Pa read and cursed, I went about my work. It wasn't long before Miss Carstairs made an appearance, lifted the lid on the stew I was making, and frowned. I supposed the meal wasn't to her liking. Well, then, she could cook it herself, and I would go sit in the shade and read a book.

Read a book? I remembered those evenings spent reading, perusing the pages of *Godey's Lady's Book*, admiring the latest fashions and deciding what crochet or embroidery patterns to copy. I had not much cared for needlework until I came here. Now I found I missed those hours of stitching and quiet contemplation.

20) CALLING NAMES

Cordelia

We had traveled without incident, passed Junction City, and had only a few miles to go before we reached Hidden Springs. I planned to camp for the night, circle around the town, and go to the house after Hiram left for his shop the next morning. Thinking of what I might say to Lucy kept me awake most of the night. I sincerely hoped Hiram had been all she imagined him to be, and that he had shown some care for his own daughter after four years of absence.

Max sensed my restlessness and called to me from the other side of the campfire. We sat up and he came to my side. We poked at the dying coals, each adding a piece of wood, and stared into the flames.

The sun was just pinking the horizon when I gave up the idea of sleep and began preparing for the day. Using Jake's wagon, I changed from my now bedraggled bloomers into the green frock I had worn for my supper at the hotel with Quinn. Then we moved through the trees to a place where we could see the house without being seen.

The stones of the house Ambrose built were perfectly laid, the building square and straight, like a fortress that might stand for centuries. Even as a toddler, he'd loved to stack things.

We waited, peering through the leaves, while Lucy gathered the eggs and milked the cow. Finally, Hiram and Ambrose left for town. As soon as they were out of sight, I hurried across the large clearing, passed the garden, and stopped in front of our old cabin. Feelings flooded me, and I had the sudden urge to look inside, to remember my mother's voice in the place I'd last heard it.

I approached the door and stood with my hand on the knob, steeling myself for a step into the past.

"Is there something I can help you with, miss?"

I whirled, confused by the unfamiliar voice, and saw a slender, pleasant-looking man in his twenties crossing the yard. He stopped a few feet from me.

"I—I used to live here," I stammered.

"You're Lucy's sister?"

"Yes, I'm returning from business out west and wanted to see how she was getting on. I'm sorry. Who are you?"

"I'm Mr. Frank Derryberry, the new schoolteacher. I'm just getting settled in and preparing for the fall term. I'll be living here in the cabin."

"I'm sorry for intruding. I didn't think of anyone living here."

"It's all right. I've not moved in yet. You may take a look around. I'll go into town and work at the school. Shall I tell Lucy you're here?"

"No, I'll surprise her."

"Very well, Miss Pierce. Perhaps I'll see you later."

"Yes," I said.

I sighed when he left. I stood for a few minutes outside the door and finally decided not to enter. The cabin was someone else's now, and place was not important: Ma was always with me. I fingered the locket containing strands of her hair and headed for the house.

I knocked at the back door. "Lucy!"

"Delia," she called out from somewhere inside.

My heart raced on hearing my childhood nickname, the one she quit using when she started resenting me.

She flung open the door and threw her arms around me. "Come in. Pa and Ambrose are already gone to town."

"I saw them leave. And I met Mr. Derryberry." I laughed. "I'll bet his students will have fun with that name. Lucky for him he's Frank instead of Harry Derryberry."

Lucy's face was alive with laughter. "That is just like you, Delia."

She pulled me inside and offered me coffee.

"Just water," I said.

We settled at the table, and Lucy began cranking the handle of the butter churn. "At least, I don't have to shake a jar until the butter comes like I used to."

"That is an improvement."

"So, did you find him?"

I knew she meant Quinn. "I did."

"And?"

"We talked, and it was awkward, and I was leaving. Then Bob Sims—do you remember him from the stage?"

"If you mean that handsome fellow you labelled a rude oaf, I do. He was there?"

"Yes. It seems his father had discovered the gold in that particular location and the place was named after him, Sims Gulch. Anyway, Bob figured out I was the girl from the stage."

"Why did he have to figure that out?"

"I was dressed as a boy so I wouldn't call attention to myself. There are maybe two or three white women for every thousand men. Anyway, he stopped me and knocked my hat off and my hair came down. A crowd gathered while he heckled me. Then Quinn, that's what I decided to call my father, showed up and chased Sims off. He escorted me down the mountain to Denver City where I met up with Miz Wilma and headed back east with her. That's when Max showed up."

"Who's Max?"

"A friend I met when I ran away that time."

I was deep in my story when the outside kitchen door banged open, and Hiram roared into the room, Ambrose behind him.

"What's this guttersnipe doing in my house?" Hiram shouted.

I stood, ready to slip past him and out the door he'd come in when he grabbed my arm, clamping down so hard I thought the bone would break.

I screamed. "Turn me loose."

"Pa," Ambrose said. "Let her go."

He did, giving me a hard shove.

I stumbled backward and fell. Seeing his boot come at me, I rolled. He missed me and lost his balance. Staggering, he caught himself on a chair and whirled to take another shot at me when Mrs. Collins and Mr. Derryberry raced through the back door.

"Hiram, stop!" Mrs. Collins shouted.

Mr. Derryberry crossed to Hiram and touched his shoulder. "Settle down, old boy. She's not worth the trouble hurting her will cause you."

Hiram's eyes blazed with anger. He was shaking and pulling away. "I'll take care of that slut."

Max came through the door, pistol in hand. "You won't touch her."

Jake, his face white and eyes wide, followed Max, a rifle in his hands.

Hiram swiped the back of his hand across his mouth and glared at me. "You got two men panting after you, do you, bitch?"

My heart squeezed into a tight ball. All the names he'd called me for the thirteen years I'd lived with him welled up in me, almost choking me.

"Stop," Lucy cried. "Don't talk to Delia that way."

Ambrose reached down and helped me to my feet. "Are you all right?"

I nodded, unable to speak.

"She's in my house. I'll talk to her any way I like," Hiram roared.

Mrs. Collins tried to insert a voice of reason. "She'll leave soon enough. Until then, be civil. You don't want word of this quarrel to leak out. You have your engagement to Miss Carstairs to think about."

Something about his reputation being soiled stopped him.

"I want to go to," Lucy said. "Can I come with you, Delia?"

"No," Hiram roared. "No. I have plans for you."

"I don't like your plans, Pa. I don't want to get married for years and years. And I don't ever want to have so many babies I die from doing it."

"Let her go," Mrs. Collins urged. "It's for the best. Miss Carstairs will want to be the sole mistress of her house. No woman wants to share her authority with another."

Hiram's chest was heaving like he was about to explode. "Go on. Get out. You're no better than your sister. You'll end up a tramp, just like her. You're no daughter of mine, so don't come crawling back here when you have a string of bastards and no way to feed them."

"Come, Lucy, I'll help you gather your things," Ambrose said.

"She's leaving here with nothing but what she's got on. I own everything in this house, and she's taking nothing with her."

Jake and Max stood on either side of the door until I was outside.

Ambrose followed them out, his arm around Lucy. He walked with us to the wagon hidden in the trees to say his goodbyes.

21) GOODBYE TO A DREAM

Lucy

I clung to Ambrose as we followed Delia to her wagon.

"I'm sorry, Luce," he said.

We came to a stop, and I slid my arms around his neck. "Oh, Ambrose, I'm the one who is sorry. You'll be all alone, and I miss you already. I'll never see you again."

"Sure, you will. I'm certain to get to Westport sometime in the next few years."

On impulse, I turned to Delia. "Can Ambrose come with us?"

"If he wants to," she said, "but it's a quick decision." She glanced anxiously at the house. "We need to leave."

I looked into Ambrose's eyes. "Please, come."

Ambrose shook his head. "Not now, Lucy. I'll come when the time is right for me. Until then, we'll keep in touch. Letters, again. Okay?"

"Okay." I sniffled and wiped away tears.

Ambrose let go of me, his eyes moist. Blinking, he took Delia's hand. "Take care of our sister."

"I will," Delia said and stepped forward, her arms going around us and ours around her.

We stood together, united, brother and sisters, a precious moment I knew I would remember the rest of my life.

Ambrose let go and stepped back. "Delia is right. You need to leave."

We climbed into the wagon. Delia drove. The younger of her two friends rode ahead of us while the other followed behind, looking back, making sure we weren't being followed.

I didn't worry about that. Pa had given his opinion of me. Thinking of all the times I had defended him to Delia and Aunt Hannah, had told them how wrong they were, I felt so ashamed.

I touched Delia's arm. "I'm sorry for every mean thing I ever said to you and Aunt Hannah. Pa is just as bad as you said. Please forgive me."

Delia gave me a sideways look. "I understand. After all, I traveled clear across Kansas Territory to find my father, a man I didn't even know."

I cried for the father I wanted, the father of my dreams, the father he never was and never would be.

Was there a bright spot in any of this? Maybe. I was such a big disappointment that Pa might forget about ever sending for Ella and Jennie.

And what would I say to my sisters? I imagined their faces, happy to see me and then sad when I told them why I was back. After all the rosy pictures of the life we might have with Pa, would they believe what I said happened, or would they doubt me as I had doubted Delia?

I shivered, my heart breaking at the task ahead.

Delia gathered the reins in one hand and reached her other to squeeze mine. "We have each other," she said, "and someday, Ambrose will join us. He promised."

.

ABOUT THE AUTHOR

Hazel Hart has been writing since she was a teenager. Her short stories and first four novels have a contemporary setting. However, with the Pierce Family Saga, she has returned to a childhood love for frontier fiction. Hazel's stories, short or long, contemporary or historical, all center on the themes of faith, family, and friendship. To learn more about books in the Pierce Family, visit her blog at https://piercefamilysaga.com.

Made in the USA
Monee, IL
09 September 2024

65340612R00092